The Awakening

The Morton Family Saga

Bonnie Poirier

Copyright © 2022 by Bonnie Poirier

All rights reserved.

No portion of this book may be reproduced, scanned or distributed in any printed or electronic form without written permission from the publisher or author, except for the use of brief quotations in a book review.

All names, characters and incidents portrayed in this story are fictitious and a product of the author's imagination. No identification with actual persons (living or deceased), places buildings and products is intended be should be inferred.

Cover by: JS Designs Covers

Edited by: VB Proofreads

Published by: Bonnie Poirier

First Edition

E-Book ISBN: 978-1-7778989-7-0

Paperback ISBN: 978-1-7778689-8-7

Contents

1. Chapter One — 1
2. Chapter Two — 6
3. Chapter Three — 14
4. Chapter Four — 19
5. Chapter Five — 27
6. Chapter Six — 32
7. Chapter Seven — 36
8. Chapter Eight — 39
9. Chapter Nine — 44
10. Chapter Ten — 47
11. Chapter Eleven — 51
12. Chapter Twelve — 55
13. Chapter Thirteen — 59
14. Chapter Fourteen — 63
15. Chapter Fifteen — 67
16. Chapter Sixteen — 72

17.	Chapter Seventeen	78
18.	Chapter Eighteen	83
19.	Chapter Nineteen	88
20.	Chapter Twenty	93
21.	Chapter Twenty-One	96
22.	Chapter Twenty-Two	100
23.	Chapter Twenty-Three	104
24.	Chapter Twenty-Four	108
25.	Chapter Twenty-Five	111
26.	Chapter Twenty-Six	116
27.	Chapter Twenty-Seven	120
28.	Chapter Twenty-Eight	124
29.	Chapter Twenty-Nine	129
30.	Chapter Thirty	133
31.	Chapter Thirty-One	136
32.	Chapter Thirty-Two	140
	Epilogue	144
	Excerpt from The Arrangement	148
	Acknowledgments	154
	About Author	155
	Also By	156

Chapter One

GAVIN

My boots crunched in the fresh snow, the sound loud in the stillness of the cold evening. I stepped with care, knowing that a hard-packed sheet of ice had formed beneath. It didn't matter how many times I shoveled the path from the barn; the snowfall was relentless this high in the mountains. The only thing more oppressive than the endless snowfall was the bone-chilling cold. When I'd come to Montana to escape my family and the failed expansion of my company, I hadn't realized how long the days would be or how hard I'd have to work.

Sure, I had worked on a ranch in Texas, but the elements had worked in my favor more often than not, and the ranch hands were more experienced. Fewer people knew what they were doing here in Montana. My brothers and I had started from scratch a few years ago, and we'd been struggling to get reliable workers ever since.

I'd been asked to step in when our ranch manager up and left. We didn't have anyone to fill the role, and since I was the only brother without a wife or kids, I'd take over the responsibilities.

The sun had set while I was in the barn bedding the horses down for the night. They were the only tolerable part of being here. They never argued, and I could talk to them about my problems or rant about how inexperienced everyone was around here without the threat of gossip.

I took a deep breath of the crisp mountain air, the little hairs in my nose freezing from the invasion of cold. The one thing about mountain air in winter was that it had a way of cleansing a person's frustrations. I rounded the corner to the cabin, finding light from the kitchen window casting across the snow.

I hadn't left that on.

The single-person log cabin had been built long ago out of hand-hewn logs and had to be maintained every spring. It was the oldest structure on the ranch. With just a kitchen and a bedroom, it was easy to heat using the firewood I chopped specifically for the purpose. I climbed the stairs, noticing the faint outline of footprints on the steps.

Was someone inside?

Very few people knew of this cabin. I opened the door as quietly as I could while I knocked the snow off my boots. I stepped inside and slipped off my winter coat and hung it on the hook. The house was warm, a fire burning in the hearth. A soft humming that came from the kitchen was the only sound besides the crackle of logs. The sweet melody eased my nerves, disarming me. My footsteps were deliberate as I side-stepped a known squeaky floorboard and followed the sound.

In the kitchen, a woman with long fiery red hair stood in front of the stove, her back to me. Hair as vibrant as the sky when the late summer sun set on the horizon swished across her back as her hips swayed to the rhythm of whatever she was listening to in the earbuds nestled in her ears. I smiled, realizing my quiet approach had been unnecessary. The upset of a home invasion was long forgotten as I admired her perfect, round ass that hugged tightly in her jeans and the long, slender legs that acted as a pedestal for the goddess-like woman in front of me.

I leaned on the archway, folding my arms across my chest. "What are you doing in my house?"

The swaying stopped as she froze in place. She shifted her bare feet on the tile and turned, looking at me. Her green eyes were as big as dinner plates, her body rigid like she was trying to decide if she should attack or scream and run.

But there was only one way out.

And I was between her and the only exit. She looked at the door, then she looked back at me.

Scream it was.

My eardrums vibrated as a scream piercing enough to start an avalanche threatened to shatter them. "Hey, hey. Lady, stop screaming."

Closing the gap between us, I reached out to touch her shoulder, a move meant to soothe her, but the second I made contact, my cheek stung, and I felt the wet warmth of whatever she was cooking splatter on my face and nose.

Okay, so I'd missed the wooden spoon she had in her hand, but I was intimately familiar with it now.

She stopped screaming with the shock of hitting me. I couldn't deny my ears were happy for the silence.

I wiped what I realized was tomato sauce from my face with the sleeve of my work shirt. "What are you doing here?" I asked through gritted teeth.

This woman didn't look much over twenty. Her features were delicate, and her skin as smooth as porcelain. She looked like a doll.

A doll with a wicked arm.

"Matt said I could stay here for a while." Her voice was soft, and she let her gaze drop to the floor.

"Who?" The name wasn't familiar to me, but maybe he was a local who knew about this place but didn't realize I'd moved in.

"Matt Riley. He's a ranch hand here and a friend of mine." She took a step back and bumped into the stove. "Sorry," she said as she turned to the gas range.

Despite her wooden-spoon wielding skills, it was difficult to feel threatened by a woman who apologized to inanimate objects. She would be a harmless house guest for the night, of that I was convinced. Besides, I hadn't seen a vehicle in the driveway. The ranch hand must have dropped her off. And I wasn't about to send her out into the cold, dark night alone.

"Now that I know why you're here, will you tell me who you are?" Moving to the table, I sat and waited for her to respond.

"Elyse Bowers. I live around here."

"You related to Hank Bowers?" Leaning forward, I waited for her reply. I'd heard things about that family over the years. They were notorious recluses who, despite keeping to themselves, had a reputation that preceded them, and not for the right reasons.

"Yes, he's my father ..." She hesitated. "Do you work with Matt?" she asked, changing the topic.

"More like he works for me."

Her eyes lit up in silent recognition. They were still wide, but not as full of fear as they had been. "You must be one of the Morton brothers, then. Mr. Morton, I—I can't go back home." Her cheeks flushed, turning the tip of her nose red, and with a quiver of her chin, tears welled in her eyes. "Please, don't make me go back. Please don't." Her words were a pleading whisper.

The poor girl looked like she would collapse at any moment. I stepped to the table and pulled out a chair for her, indicating that she should take a seat. She shook her head, shuffling over to lean against the counter instead. So much fear existed in her. Even when I'd done my best to make it obvious that I posed no threat. But why? What kind of hell was she running from?

"You're the daughter who was supposed to get married, aren't you?" Leaning my elbows on the table, I waited for the answer I already knew.

Talk had filtered through the mountain that things weren't good between her and the fiancé, but I needed to know how bad they were. If I was going to get myself into trouble, which I had a tendency of, I wanted to know more about what I was up against first.

"I assure you, Mr. Morton—"

"Gavin," I cut her off.

"Oh, Gavin, I promise you I won't be any trouble. Nobody knows where I am. I've been gone for days, but I ran out of money for a hotel. They have probably given up even looking for me by now." She picked up a dish towel, wringing it in her hands, before bringing it to her chest, her knuckles white as if she were hanging on to it for dear life.

"I won't send you back. But what's your plan after you wear out your welcome here?" I was only joking, but she couldn't stay forever.

The blank expression on her face made it clear that she hadn't thought much about what to do next. She'd probably been more concerned with finding somewhere to hide out of the cold.

"I need to get out of the state, and then I don't care where I go." She crossed her arms as a tear fell down her cheek.

CHAPTER ONE 5

There was no denying her determination. What she was up against must have been bad if she was willing to start over somewhere new to escape. I needed to know more. I still wasn't sure if I should be getting mixed up in what she had going on.

The entire mountain was curious about her father and the community he had started years ago, but idle gossip in these small towns was often inaccurate. Although from what I'd heard, I wouldn't want to stick around any more than she did. I had a job to do here, keeping the ranch in order, but I found my need to help solidifying as I regarded the young woman who was little more than a stranger—a beautiful one, and one in need.

Chapter Two

ELLIE

I could see it in his eyes, the hesitation. He was going to make me go home, and I bet he would take me there tonight. Of course he would. I was asking a lot of a man I'd just met. My heart raced in my chest, no longer out of fear of him, but because my return was inevitable. No one local was willing to help me. My father had made sure of that. Gavin was my only chance. A chance I hadn't even known I had until he'd startled me half to death. But from the look on his face, that slight chance was, in reality, no chance at all.

There had to be another option.

It was nobody's business but mine why I wanted to escape my wedding. But if I was going to convince him to help me, I might have to make it his business. Although I wanted to avoid doing that for as long as I could. I'd narrowly escaped marrying a monster, but as I took in Gavin's dark hair, his tall, broad frame, and his muscular body, I thought—no, I knew—that if anyone could protect me, it would be him.

But he had no duty to do so.

I had to remember that.

Still, along with the hesitation in his eyes, there was an undeniable kindness. A warmth emanated from him that heated me to the core. Never mind that he was devilishly handsome in his plaid shirt and blue jeans. I couldn't help but stare as he sat at his kitchen table, studying me. Surely wondering how on earth he'd been stuck with me. As I watched him, he rolled up his sleeves, careful to avoid the sauce, and revealed his tan, sinewy forearms.

I'd done enough gawking. I needed to state my case. I shook my head to clear the thoughts of him and spoke. "Mr. Morton. Gavin. I have nowhere to go. Let's leave it at that. If you'll let me stay the tonight, I'll have Matt pick me up in the morning." My voice shook. I would have to figure out a new plan to evade my father.

"You can stay." He paused, his expression thoughtful. "As long as you need to." The kind words were evidence of what I already knew from his gaze, but hearing them spoken aloud made my heart soar. If I knew him better, nothing could have stopped me from lunging at him and wrapping him in the tightest hug ever.

"Are you sure?"

He nodded with a slight grin on his face.

"Thank you." I turned back to the stove in an attempt to conceal my growing smile before his all-too-handsome gaze threatened to overheat me where I stood. As I stirred the meat sauce, which I was sure was on the verge of burning, I could see him watching me out of the corner of my eye. I lifted the spoon to my mouth for a taste to see if I'd saved it in time. I had.

"Do you happen to be making enough for two people to eat?" His voice had changed from concerned to teasing.

That was it.

My ticket to freedom lay in the belly of this man. Judging by the frozen dinners I'd spotted in the freezer earlier, he was in desperate need of some home-cooked meals.

Not to mention his cabin looked like it could use a deep clean. I'd make his life so easy, he'd be begging me not to leave.

"Of course, I do. It's almost ready. Go wash up, and when you're back, supper will be on the table." A rogue tear fell and landed on my shirt. I was so damn grateful for his generosity and for the normalcy of this conversation.

"Don't cry. It's all going to be fine." He walked over to me and wiped the tear's trail from my cheek. My body was acutely aware of his closeness, the rough but gentle feel of his thumb on my cheek remaining even after his hand fell away.

"Let's just say you picked the right remote cabin to break in to." With that, he turned and headed out of the room.

His words were kind, and his actions thoughtful. It was totally opposite from the rumors I'd heard about the Mortons. Or the unpleasant gossip that had been swirling around the area since he'd arrived. Though no one quite knew what had happened down south, the term embezzlement had been thrown around a lot. The pain etched into each line of his face came to mind as I dished up the plates. Or maybe it was loneliness. It radiated from him—from the slump of his shoulders to the hurt in his eyes. Even his good looks couldn't conceal the anguish. Rumors were just that, rumors. I was sure there were plenty floating around about me these days too, if they hadn't been my whole life. Regardless of the truth, as long as he let me stay, I would do everything in my power to make him not regret it.

When he returned to the kitchen, he walked up behind me and sniffed over my shoulder. "That smells amazing."

"It was the best I could do. You need groceries, but I managed to find enough for spaghetti and meat sauce." I turned and smiled at him.

"It's my favorite, and the only thing I actually know how to cook with any kind of competency. I will always have the ingredients for it. Mind you, it never smells that good when I'm making it," he tossed out as he walked back to the table.

I set the plates on the table. "Well, thank you. I'll have to remember that." His eyes regarded me hungrily. Or was he just looking at the food in my hands? I couldn't be sure as I set his plate in front of him, and I took a seat across the table. "Please, eat."

He swirled his fork in the heaping mound of spaghetti I'd dished out for him and shoveled his first bite into his mouth like he hadn't seen a decent meal in months. His eyes popped open as he groaned. When he'd swallowed back his mouthful, he shook his head. "You're going to have to teach me your ways. This is too good."

"No, not going to happen. If I reveal my secrets, then what reason will you have to keep me around?" My tone was light and teasing for the first time.

He set his fork on the side of his plate. "I'm sure your skills aren't limited to spaghetti alone."

The way he studied me made my heart race and my mouth dry up.

Water. I needed water. I slipped out of the chair and raced to the sink. I pulled two glasses from the cupboard and filled the first, then drained it completely before filling it again.

He let out a low chuckle before I returned to the table with a glass of water for each of us.

"So, are you going to tell me what exactly made you run?"

Stopping midbite, I looked up from my plate. It wasn't the supper conversation I'd wished for, but he had every right to know why I'd broken into his home.

"Are you sure you want to know? The story might ruin your favorite supper for you." I couldn't help but smile at him before I put the forkful of pasta into my mouth.

"I think I can handle it."

"Consider yourself warned."

He took another huge bite and chewed with a nod.

I sighed, setting my fork down. I wasn't going to get away keeping the full story from him. "My father arranged for me to marry Ray Hamish. We were supposed to be married next month. Ray was affectionate. Much too affectionate, as it turns out." Pushing my food around on the plate, I hesitated to continue. Gavin was a stranger; he didn't need to know my life story. Let alone parts of it I was too embarrassed or ashamed to tell.

"He pushed for intimacy sooner than I expected. He said it would be fine since we were getting married. Well, one time turned into two, and then we couldn't keep our hands off each other, and…" I couldn't tell him the rest. Not now.

He swallowed back his bite, and when he didn't say anything, I knew I was expected to continue.

"When a girl who has been sheltered from men her entire life and taught purity culture is faced with a situation like that, she's not prepared. At all." I was all too aware that I was telling the story like it wasn't my own, but somehow, distancing myself from it made it easier. "So, I guess, in short, I'm running away from pressures I wasn't prepared for."

But there was one thing I couldn't run away from.

One thing that would follow me no matter how far I went. It was the reason I needed to distance myself from Ray as fast as I could. The baby in my womb may have been only a whisper of life inside me, but it depended on me. And that meant not letting a manipulative and cruel man like Ray anywhere near me.

"How old are you, Ellie?" Gavin asked, looking at me another with another fork over-wound with spaghetti at the ready.

"Twenty-three."

"Let me get this straight. You're running away because your fiancé wanted to have sex with you?" He snickered a little as he asked.

"Like I said, I was sheltered," I snapped. My short reply was unwise, considering he had the ability to kick me out into the cold winter's night. But he was making fun of me. I hated it when people assumed I was a dumb mountain girl who needed a man to survive. I sat up and stared straight into his eyes. "Just so you know, I had plans to go to veterinary school. I had scholarships in place, but I couldn't get the rest of the money together. My father was against it, and he refused to let me work to save up to go. While I may be inexperienced, I'm not dumb, Mr. Morton."

"Forgive me, Elyse, I never meant to imply that you were." His words sounded sincere and remained soft, even as my tongue became sharp.

Pushing my plate away, I rested my elbows on the table and immediately removed them. That was one thing that would immediately get Ray's dander up.

"I guess what I meant to say was there must be more to it than that. More than a man wanting to have sex with you to make you run." Gavin leaned back in his chair, his attention fixed to me like he was waiting for an answer.

"He's... controlling." I touched my wrist as I remembered how Ray had grabbed me when I told him about the baby. How he'd accused me of trying to ruin his reputation in the community because people would do the math and realize we'd conceived out of wedlock. How he made it seem like it had all been my idea—how he'd tried to gaslight me into believing it had been—and how he'd even gone as far as calling me a little slut and a temptress. I closed my eyes and shook my head. It was too much to say out loud.

"You don't have to continue Ellie. I think I understand." Gavin leaned forward and put his hand over mine. The warmth of his palm radiated through me.

I hadn't been touched like that before. Ray was always gruff. I didn't think he'd ever loved me. He only wanted the status that came along with marrying into my family. And here was a man who had known me for less than an hour and had already treated me with more kindness than I'd ever experienced. It was almost disorienting. Like it was too good to be true. But I hoped I could take him at his word. That he wouldn't expect more of me than I could give.

"But I have to ask. Should I be concerned about repercussions?"

I shook my head. "I can't imagine why. My family is disgraced, and Ray will surely have a new, unsuspecting fiancée in the next few weeks. Given the history of the community, there will be plenty of women looking to lick his wounds after my disappearance. He will be deemed the innocent party, and I'll be accused of leading him astray." I hoped, by leaving, Ray was getting exactly what he wanted. The reality of what we had done would disappear right along with me.

"Well, that's more than a little messed up." He stood from his chair and cleared the table.

We cleaned up after the meal in silence. It was strange. Not the silence, but having the help of a man. He even washed the dishes while I dried and put them away. I'd never witnessed anything like it before. The kitchen wasn't a man's place in the community I grew up in.

"Ellie, how long have you been gone from home?" Gavin asked when the last dish was put away.

"Three days. I was staying in the motel by the highway, but it was too risky. Someone would eventually spot me. Besides, I was running out of money." Leaning against the counter, I waited for his response. He didn't say anymore, only nodded.

It was late, and all I wanted to do was go to bed. "Can you show me to my room?" I asked. The cabin wasn't big, and I was sure the spare bedroom wouldn't be much bigger than a closet, but I didn't care. All I needed was a place to rest my head.

"Come on." He motioned for me to follow him. The hall was more of an alcove with a door on either side. "You can in sleep here," he said, pushing the one on the left open. I surveyed the room. His clothes were hanging in the open closet, his jeans from earlier discarded in the laundry basket at the foot of the bed. There was a wristwatch on the bedside table. All his things were in the room.

He'd led me to his room.

"Where will you sleep?"

He tipped his head, his brows furrowed as his lips twisted into a smirk. Brushing past me he flopped down on the mattress and patted it before folding his hands behind his head.

"Tell me, Ellie"—I'd left that nickname behind in my childhood but something about the way it rolled off his tongue made my heart hammer in my chest—"Do you prefer to be the little spoon or the big spoon?" He waggled his eyebrows.

I burst out laughing. It felt good to laugh. "Gavin, you're funny. As if I would spend the night in the same bed as a man I just met."

"I ain't joking, princess. The couch isn't fit to sleep on, and I won't sleep on the floor."

He was right. The couch was more of a loveseat. It wasn't long enough for even me to stretch out on. And I couldn't push a man out of his only bed. "You don't keep a cot around? I would be more than happy to sleep on that."

Gavin shook his head.

"I can sleep on the floor," I said.

"Look, it's winter. The cabin is only heated by the wood stove, and the floor gets cold in the night. I promise this is only an offer for sleep."

I looked into his eyes. They were soft and held concern, filling me with an odd sense of peace. That wasn't something I had felt for the last few days. Closing my eyes, I sighed and nodded.

He sat up on his elbows and smiled. "No counterargument? Excellent, it's settled then. You're the big spoon. I'll keep my hands to myself. You have my word."

He rolled to the other side of the bed and turned his back to me, leaving me plenty of room to climb in next to him. I hesitated for a moment before crossing the room and pulling a blanket off the foot of the bed. I bunched it up to form a makeshift wall between us and climbed in.

He looked over his shoulder at me and winked. "Just try not to take advantage of me in the middle of the night, will you?"

Our laughter filled the tiny room for a moment, but then silence descended as we settled in. The room was still and quiet enough for me to hear his breathing deepen as he fell fast asleep. I pulled some of the blanket from the barrier over my body, and closed my eyes, and even though I had no right to feel the way I did, for the first time in ages, I felt safe.

Chapter Three

GAVIN

A loud banging shook me from my peaceful slumber. Who could be awake at this hour? Who cared? I nestled back into my pillow, my arm tightening around something—no, someone.

I cracked one eye open, the realization that I wasn't alone overcoming me. I had an armed wrapped firmly around Ellie, and she was snuggled up tight against me.

Looked like I was the big spoon, after all.

It had been so long since I'd held anyone, and she looked so peaceful in my arms. Maybe needed to be held as much as I needed to do the holding. I didn't care who was at the door. They hadn't banged again, so maybe it had been a dream.

Just as I closed my eyes again, ready to soak in the feeling of a beautiful woman in my arms, the door flew open with a bang. Ellie startled awake, looking between her father and me in a half-awake state of confusion. I pulled her closer.

"Morton, what are you doing to my daughter?" His voice boomed out.

Guess it wasn't a dream.

"Hank, what are you doing breaking into my home?"

He put his hands on his hips, pulling back his jacket as he did and revealing a holster on his hip. I didn't dare move. The bright metal grip of his gun shone in the moonlight.

CHAPTER THREE

"Elyse, get out of that bed at once." She twitched in my arms but didn't move. The man was a force. He was as wide as he was tall, the skin on his cruel looking face ruddy. Word had it he ruled his home with an iron fist, and anyone on the mountain who was outside of his twisted community had the sense to avoid him.

Anyone except me.

"Now, Hank, come on, let's talk about this. No need for shouting." I took care removing my arm from Ellie and rolled out of bed to stand face-to-face with the man as two other men appeared behind him.

"Elyse, get up, you've had your fun." He spat. "Ray told us you were gone. Said you'd be out sleeping around. I almost didn't believe him." He shook his head as Elyse sat up in the bed. "I thought I taught you better than this. A man needs his woman at home waiting on him hand and foot. Not off sleeping with some makeshift city boy out here flashing his cash and pretending to be a rancher." The man puffed out his chest. "Like your mother. Now she's a wife. Come on you trash, get out of that bed."

He could trash talk me all he wanted, but as I looked back at Ellie, the sadness in her eyes broke me. I'd promised her she could stay for as long as she wanted. I thought she'd be safe out here.

"Don't talk to my wife like that." Who was speaking, and why did it sound like my voice?

"Your wife?" He repeated, as startled by my words as I was.

"Did I stutter?" I took a step toward him. There was no backing down. Either I'd just had the biggest stroke of genius, or I was about to get a chest full of lead. "Now, get out of my home and away from my wife." There I went, saying it again. "If you ever set foot on my property again, or make contact with Ellie, I'll have you arrested." I kept stepping until I had him backed into the living room.

"Her name is Elyse, not Ellie." Her father growled.

One more way he controlled her, I figured. "I don't come into your home and tell you what to call your wife, now do I? Besides, Ellie rolls off the tongue so much better than a stuffy name like Elyse."

"It was my mother's name." He said through gritted teeth.

"I'm sure your father called her Ellie in the bedroom, too." A chuckle escaped as I imagined this big man thinking about his parents.

Flicking the light on as I went by, I saw there was a fourth man. These must have been his sons. All three were carrying hunting rifles, and they were pointed at me, but all they were shooting was daggers as they stared at me.

Ellie was hot on my heels, and I held out my arm, keeping her behind me. These assholes weren't going to intimidate me into anything. They'd picked the wrong man. I had nothing left to lose. And I wasn't about to offer her up to them when she'd made it so clear she needed to escape.

"Married? Shacking up is more like it." One of her brothers mumbled loud enough to hear it.

"Just so you're aware, Ellie and I eloped. Where did you think she'd been these past few days? Hiding out at a hotel on the highway?" I didn't bother to suppress my smile. "We just got back from our honeymoon."

I looked over my shoulder at her from the corner of my eye. Her mouth was open wide enough to catch flies. As long as it stayed that way, and she didn't contradict me, we'd be all right.

Her father waved his hand at his minions, signaling them to lower their weapons. I turned, wrapping my arm around Ellie and pulled her tight to my side.

No time like the present to make them squirm more.

Leaning down, I tipped Ellie's chin, and she met my gaze as I winked before I pressed my mouth to hers. Her lips were soft, and delicious pressed against mine. She melted into me as I wrapped both arms around her, once again breaking my promise to keep my hands to myself. She opened her mouth, and I took the opportunity to swirl my tongue around hers.

She didn't seem to mind too much.

She was the best kisser I had ever had the privilege of kissing. At that moment, it was like the world around us fell away. It was just me and her and this kiss.

Lost in the haze that formed around us, I vaguely registered the sound of a throat clearing.

Oh right, we had an audience.

I broke the kiss and turned to face them again, but she remained close with her hand on my chest. Sparks had flown, and my world was spinning. What had I just done?

"She ain't wearing a ring."

"That's because I want to get her the best. It's being custom made by my family's jeweler in Dallas. Sent her measurements yesterday." I looked down at Ellie and smiled. "Isn't that right, sweetheart?" This was getting more far-fetched by the second. I needed her to corroborate my story.

Her eyes widened, but she mustered a nod. That would have to do.

"Elyse, is this true?" Hank's attention turned from me to his daughter.

My pulse raced, and doubt crept into my head. What would happen if she said no? They caught us in bed together. We'd had pure intentions, and nothing had happened between us, but Hank's narrow mind wouldn't accept that answer. What she was about to say would determine whether I was a dead man.

"Yes, Daddy, it's true. Gavin and I are husband and wife."

Her voice was firm and confident. If I hadn't known better, I would have believed her myself.

"I see." He stroked his chin. "Let's go home, boys." His shoulders slumped, and he glanced back at his sons. "This is going to kill your mother, Elyse. Your actions have shamed us all. I hope you're happy, because you aren't welcome in our home any longer." Hank turned and left the house, followed by his sons, who didn't give Ellie a second glance as they left.

Ellie had a death grip on my arm, and she was shaking, but she stood proud and strong beside me as they left.

"Oh, no." she whispered as she crumpled to the floor in a heap. Quiet sobs made her shoulders shake.

I gathered her in my arms and carried her to the sofa, the kneeled before her. "I'm sorry. I didn't know how else to get us out of that situation. I didn't think they would turn their backs on you. Ellie, I'm sorry."

She shook her head against my shoulder. "It's not that, that was inevitable. But I'm worried about what they're going to do once they figure out it is all a lie."

"Inevitable? But you're his daughter."

"Exactly, I'm a daughter. Unlike my brothers, I'm a liability to him. My father always made it clear I was a burden, and the only way I could fix that was to marry someone he felt was fit to join the family."

I took both her hands in mine. "You could never be a liability. Your spaghetti making skills alone make you an asset in my eyes."

She gave me a sweet smile, but it quickly faded, and the tears returned. "He chose Ray for me, and it was my duty to eventually come around to him. I was told I would learn to love eventually, even though he repulsed me from the very start. Still, I tried, Gavin, I really tried."

As her tears dried up and her sobs stopped, she told me more about the environment she was raised in. She'd been robbed. Of her happiness. Her choices. And of her self worth. She deserved a family that thought the world of her and accepted her for who she was.

Speaking of families, the chances were slim that this story wouldn't get back to mine. Elyse's mother wouldn't be the only one disappointed to hear that we'd eloped. But I supposed bringing my "wife" home for Christmas would make up for it.

"This ranch hand friend of yours, Matt. How experienced is he?"

She tipped her head at me. "He's worked on ranches his whole life. Why?"

"He's about to get a temporary promotion to ranch manager. If he can hack it, we'll see about making it permanent. That is, if you'll agree to come to Texas with me for Christmas."

She eyed me cautiously. "Are you serious?"

I nodded.

The bright smile on her face was contagious, and before I knew it, she'd thrown her arms around my neck and hugged me tight. "Thank you, Gavin. Thank you so much." She damn near knocked me off my feet with the force of her hug, her scent—something floral with a sweet hint of vanilla—invading my senses.

It looked like we were heading home together.

Me and my fake wife.

Chapter Four

ELLIE

It wasn't real. Gavin was only trying to protect me. But sitting on the sofa, snuggled under his protective arm after he had saved me from the wrath of my father made me wish we truly were a couple. While I'd dreaded the idea of being married to Ray, there was something about Gavin that made me feel the exact opposite. Giddy even. But I needed to control that feeling. It was crazy—he was a virtual stranger, and he wouldn't want me if he knew the whole truth. I rested my hand on my belly. It was still too soon for me to show.

Why he was offering this, I couldn't fathom, but going along with his plan would give me a little more time to figure out what I was going to do. But more importantly, it got me far away from Montana.

"What now?" Part of me didn't want to know because I was worried he planned to dump me off somewhere before I could get my bearings. The other part of me was scared he would want to keep up the charade.

"We pack our bags. I hadn't planned on leaving this early, but I did promise to be home for Christmas, and I won't leave you here." He tightened his arms around me. "Like it or not, wifey, you're part of the Morton family now." He shook his head. "You have no idea what you're in for." His chuckle made me smile.

"I'm going back to bed." We'd been woken in the middle of the night, and being on the lam for the last few days was catching up to me. Shifting away from Gavin, I stood and headed for the bedroom.

"Well, I suppose since it's our honeymoon, I should join you, little spoon." Gavin heaved himself off the couch and winked at me.

His words broke the tension, and I laughed, which was a virtual miracle after what had gone on earlier. "Come on, husband." I held out my hand for him. Although I'd reached for him, I was still surprised when he placed his palm in mine. We were going to have to make this look real, so this was probably a good place to start.

Lying in the bed next to him, I made no effort to keep my distance. After what we had gone through with my father—being woken in the middle of the night, all but held at gunpoint—there was an intimacy that made me crave his closeness. Tucked up against him, feeling his warmth, that safe feeling returned. He'd proven himself worthy of it. A weaker man might have crumbled under the pressure earlier. He barely knew me, and he owed me nothing, but he'd protected me even with three rifles pointed at him. The way he out-witted my father and brothers with ease was nothing short of amazing.

When I woke again, Gavin's side of the bed was empty. I wandered into the kitchen, looking for him. The pot of coffee was half full, and on the counter beside it was a note. I picked it up and read it as I went to get a coffee mug.

Ellie,

I've gone to check the cattle and make arrangements so we can leave here this afternoon.

Won't be gone long. Get ready to go.

Gavin

There wasn't much for me to get ready, but I could help Gavin. Sipping my coffee, I walked into the bedroom and opened the closet. His wardrobe was simple, all plaid western shirts and jeans. There was a suitcase tucked into the corner of the closet.

CHAPTER FOUR

I set my cup down on the bedside table, pulled the suitcase out, and flopped it on the bed to unzip it, then I folded everything neatly, hoping to avoid wrinkles.

An hour passed, and I'd packed everything I thought he might need. Staying busy helped me keep my mind off the events of the last twenty-four hours.

The door swung open, and Gavin entered the house. His dark hair was covered in snow and his cheeks were rosy from the cold. Although he looked like he had fought with a blizzard, the sight of him simultaneously put me at ease and caused my body to heat.

"I need to get out of these clothes and then we can leave." He said as he peeled off layer after layer of warm clothes, his attention catching on the bags I'd set at the door. "Did you pack my stuff?"

"I left you a change of clothes on the bed, but I packed the rest. I figured we needed to get going and it would save time." I hesitated. Was he mad that I'd gone through his things? "I hope I didn't overstep."

"Not at all. Thank you." He nodded and walked into the room to change. He left the door open, talking to me as he moved around the room. "I've been thinking. There is only one way to make sure you're safe, and I'm not sure you're going to like it. We have to actually get married."

What? He didn't even know me, and I'd broken into his house last night. "No, Gavin, you've already done too much. It was one thing to make my father think that we had eloped. But to actually go get legally married? I can't do that to you." I shook my head. We'd only just met. Would he really be willing to marry me after such a short time? Just to keep me safe?

"You aren't doing this to me Ellie, I chose this. We'll go to the courthouse and get a license. I booked us in at the justice of the peace in two hours. That'll give us enough time to get everything sorted before our flight."

"Why are you doing this?"

"Because you deserve to have a life. You can't stay in this town, and you shouldn't have to live in hiding." He came out of the bedroom, his shirt still half unbuttoned.

I sucked in a breath at the sight of his muscular chest.

Moving closer to me, Gavin brought his hand up, but before he touched my cheek, I flinched. He dropped his hand and continued buttoning his shirt.

To my surprise, he didn't ask about my reaction. Instead, he turned and walked into the kitchen.

"We should head out as soon as we can. I don't want you to stay here any longer than you have to. Your family knows where you are, so we can assume Ray does, too. It's time to go." He grabbed our bags and carried them to the truck without another word.

The drive to town was silent. I wondered what he was thinking. Did he want to get out of this? Was Gavin making the mistake of his life?

Was I?

But when Gavin pulled to a stop in front of the courthouse and looked over at me, his smile was warm and eased the fear inside me. "Ready?".

Was I ready? How ready could I be? We'd only just met. But I was ready to get out of Montana and I could think of far worse ways to accomplish that than marrying Gavin. I still didn't see how he stood to benefit from it, but I wasn't about to talk him out of it either. "Yes. Let's go."

The clerk was nice, and while we waited for her to find the paperwork we needed, Gavin wrapped his arm around my waist, just like he'd done last night with my father. Gavin knew how to charm people. Especially women from what I could tell. Just the sight of him had every woman in the office fluttering her lashes and tittering.

"Congratulations, you two." The cheery woman behind the counter said, double-checking the forms we'd filled out. Once Gavin paid, she slid the through the hole in her ticket window.

I clutched the paperwork to my chest, and we walked hand-in-hand and sat down where the clerk had told us to. I bounced my knee a few times before I caught myself and forced it to stop. My heart was racing and the marriage license in my hand shook. Gavin gently pulled it from my clutches.

He was so calm and collected. I wanted to match his energy, so I did my best to hide the nerves I was feeling from him. I took a deep breath in and held it before slowly letting it out. I straightened out my fingers, which had been clenched tightly since Gavin had taken the marriage application from me.

An old man appeared at the door across from us, holding it open for a newlywed couple to exit. He congratulated them, shaking hands with first the young man, then the woman, then they said their thanks and goodbyes, before he turned in our direction. Gavin took my hand and stood. My legs felt like they were made of lead as we crossed the hall and followed the justice of the peace into his room. If anyone had told me that I'd one day be married outside of a church, I'd have called them crazy. But there I was, about to do exactly that.

Music played softly throughout the small room. A few pews lined either side of the aisle, and the justice of the peace was flanked on either side by understated silk flowers. The relaxed atmosphere inside the room settled my doubt nominally.

"Okay, you two, let's start. Gavin come with me and Elyse, my wife, Janet will take you from here and get you all set up." The old man pointed to a woman sitting at a desk nearby, then he escorted Gavin through a set of double doors.#

The small, slender woman with perfectly coiffed gray hair and a gentle smile handed me a bouquet of silk flowers that looked like they had been around since the beginning of time. It seemed impossible for silk flowers to wilt—that was the point of using them rather than real flowers, wasn't it?—but the ones in my hand looked like they were about ready to give up on that promise. She flung the door open, revealing an altar where her husband and Gavin stood.

My hands trembled as I held the bouquet. If someone had checked my pulse, I'm sure I would have been hospitalized because I thought my heart was going to beat out of my chest. Chewing on the corner of my mouth I hoped the justice of the peace didn't pick up on how nervous I was.

More importantly, I didn't want Gavin to sense my hesitation.

I moved slowly down the aisle toward Gavin while he stared back at me, a kind smile on his face. This man was handsome, tall, and strong, and I was going to marry him. I could do worse, far worse. In fact, I almost had, but this didn't feel right. He needed to know the truth.

The whole truth.

"A marriage isn't to be entered into lightly. The two of you have decided to join your lives together. Through happy times, difficult times and through whatever else life decides to throw at you." The man droned on, and I stared at Gavin, my clammy hands draped in his open palms. I was a fraud. The justice of the peace was speaking of the challenges of marriage, the importance of the bond, and how we'd have to stick together through it all. But our marriage wasn't one that would be built on that kind of foundation. We weren't marrying for love.

"Elyse, do you take Gavin as your husband?"

I studied Gavin, looking intently into his eyes. And all I could think about was how kind he was, how ready he was to take on my troubles. Only he didn't know all the details or what, in about eight months, my life—our lives—would be like if we went through with this marriage. Fake or not, I couldn't put him through it. He gave my hands a little squeeze of encouragement, but I pulled them away.

"No, I—I can't. I can't do this to you, Gavin." I ran down the aisle and pushed my way through the double doors. I didn't stop running until I found the women's bathroom.

I turned on the tap and splashed my face with cool water. I gripped the sides of the sink and leaned over it, sucking in a few deep breaths to calm myself.

The bathroom door squeaked open. "Are you going to tell me what's happening?" Gavin's low voice called out to me.

I shut my eyes and swallowed hard. That was the problem. I didn't want to tell him. "I can't marry you. It was nice of you to offer, and I appreciate it, but I can't get you mixed up in this." I turned to look at him, shaking the water from my hands, pleading with him to agree without asking more questions.

He stepped inside the restroom, letting the door fall closed behind him. "Ellie, I'm already mixed up in it. I don't understand what you're so worried about. We've got a flight to catch, so let's just get this over with, okay?" He reached his hand out for me to take.

"Gavin, I'm pregnant."

If he was panicked, his face didn't show it. His expression didn't even change. I expected shock, outrage, a stern 'how could you' even. But instead, he regarded me with a gentle look, calm and silent. The judgment I'd been conditioned to expect absent.

But maybe his silence was speaking volumes.

Taking a deep breath, he nodded. "Okay. We'll have to work on our story. Come on, let's get married. We can deal with this later."

That was it? After all, that build up? All the tension I felt? The guilt brewing in my gut didn't disappear but had been reduced to a simmer.

I shook my head and took the hand he still offered to me. "Where did you come from, Gavin Morton?"

"Texas." He said with a straight face, and I couldn't help but laugh. He pulled me to him, his eyes locked on mine, and for a brief moment, I thought he might kiss me. But instead, he turned and led us out of the bathroom, and back to the altar.

The old man stood from his chair. "You're back."

Gavin gave him a curt nod. "Sorry, sir. We're ready now."

The old man smiled, the laugh lines around his face crinkling. "Where was I? Oh right. Elyse, do you take Gavin as your lawfully wedded husband?"

"I do." My voice was strong, and even though I knew this was a marriage of convenience, the moment felt special.

"Gavin, do you take Elyse as your lawfully wedded wife?"

"I do." He didn't hesitate and never took his eyes off me.

"By the power given to me by the state of Montana, I am pleased to pronounce you husband and wife. Mr. Morton, you may kiss your bride."

Gavin's eyes grew wide, and he hesitated for a split second before he leaned in and kissed me. The magnetic pull between us from the night before returned, and what was intended to be a quick peck turned into so much more. Gavin laced his fingers in my hair and pulled me closer, his mouth fusing more securely to mine. The kiss deepened, but I couldn't tell you who was in control. He groaned against my lips as I ran my hands up his back. He could have whisked me away anywhere in that moment and I would have gone without question or hesitation.

Janet clapped from behind us. "Save something for the honeymoon, you two."

We broke our kiss, and I searched his eyes, looking for clues as to how he felt about the connection we'd just shared. I half expected to see regret, but he only smiled down at me. I couldn't help but return it, feeling more at peace than I had in a long time. As I signed the paper that made us legally husband and wife, there was a tiny part of me that wished it hadn't gone down the way it had. I wondered, if we'd met under different circumstances, would we have married for the right reasons?

No, don't go there.

I pushed those thoughts from my mind. It had happened the way it had, and it would end when the time was right. I owed him for my safety and my freedom, and the best way I could repay him for his overwhelming act of kindness was by keeping a level head about this whole situation.

I was Gavin Morton's wife on paper, but nothing more.

Chapter Five

ELIE

We arrived at the airport, and I—a bit bewilderedly—followed Gavin to a private plane. First class would have been more than I could have imagined. A coach seat, crammed between Gavin and a woman with a crying baby, would have been perfect. I'd never flown before, and always hoped I one day could. But a private plane? The nerves returned. How different was Gavin's life from mine? Was he used to this kind of luxury? Maybe I was more of an inexperienced mountain girl than I'd realized. After all, I hadn't even been out of state before.

Gavin turned back to me. "Are you going to stand there all day?"

"This is a private plane, Gavin."

"Would you rather fly commercial?" He didn't wait for me to respond. "We can if it would make you feel more comfortable, but it seems kind of pointless when the plane is already here. Tony had to leave his family early this morning to get here."

"I'm sorry, I was just surprised. I haven't flown before, let alone taken a private plane."

Gavin doubled back, giving me a gentle push toward the plan. "There's a first time for everything. Go on, we have things to discuss." He grinned when I finally got my feet unstuck and moved toward the plane. How was he so relaxed about all this? Our worlds had been flipped upside down, and he acted like flying in a private jet with his new wife to surprise his family was an every-day occurrence.

He followed close behind as I walked up the steps to the open door of the plane.

The seats were leather, the color of buttercream. A couch ran along the one side of the cabin, with a table and chairs across the aisle. There was a large television on the back wall, and a bar in the corner with a smiling flight attendant standing behind it. The plane was fancier than the home I'd grown up in. Who was I kidding? It was fancier than any home I'd ever set foot in. "Whose plane is this?"

"It belongs to my family. Since I fly back and forth to Montana so frequently, it was the practical thing to do." Gavin said nonchalantly.

"So practical." I didn't see the practicality in it at all, but I nodded and at him, anyway, moving my head in a way I hoped would be convincing.

His laughter reverberated through the cabin of the plane. "I guess it's somewhat impractical, given the way you grew up. But it's been our normal for quite a while."

I stood in the aisle. He was right about that. It wasn't something I was accustomed to at all. Again, why would a man like him, who had the world at his fingertips and could jet off anywhere he liked in a private plane, tie himself to me?

He pointed to one of the chairs at the table. "Have a seat over there and buckle up."

A man in what I assumed was a pilot's uniform walked over to Gavin and shook his hand. "Mr. Morton, it's always a pleasure to have you aboard."

"Thank you for making this unscheduled trip, Tony. At least there won't be a return flight any time soon." The men laughed.

"Ellie, this is Tony. He's our family pilot," Gavin said.

I nodded at him, and he gave me a warm smile.

Gavin stretched an arm in my direction, then introduced me. "Tony, this is Ellie. My wife."

Tony's smile disappeared, and he blinked, a look of shock, or maybe disbelief, descending on his face.

He schooled his expression so quickly I didn't think Gavin had even noticed it. "Ellie, it's nice to meet you." He stuck his hand out and I shook it.

"And you Tony."

"It's her first flight, so make sure it's a good one." Gavin patted Tony on the back, and they shared another laugh before the pilot walked away. Was there anyone my husband couldn't charm?

"You have a family pilot?" I narrowed my eyes at him, trying to keep the smirk off my face.

He shrugged. "Of course, don't you?"

I shook my head and sat in my seat, trying to hide a moan of pleasure as I melted into the soft leather, and fumbled with my belt. He rounded the table and slid into the seat next to me before taking the belt from my hands. He clicked it closed and tightened it around my hips. "I know how to buckle a seat belt, Gavin."

"You could've fooled me." He smirked, then, instead of returning to his seat, he buckled up next to me. Butterflies fluttered in my stomach. I tried to convince myself it was because I was about to fly for the first time, and that it had nothing to do with how close Gavin was. The kiss we'd shared at the courthouse replayed in my mind, as I sat back and tried to calm myself with a few deep breaths. I'd always envisioned being allowed to travel once I was a married woman, but I never imagined I'd be doing so with my fake husband while carrying a baby that wasn't his.

The plane rolled forward, and I jumped in my seat. Gavin reached over and took my hand in his and held it while the aircraft hurtled down the runway and lifted off into the air. My stomach flip-flopped, whether from the takeoff or the touch of Gavin's hand, I wasn't sure. It was equal parts exhilarating and terrifying.

"We could join the mile high club once the seat belt signs are off. Consummate this marriage before we get to Texas." Gavin wiggled his eyebrows and gave me a sly grin.

"No." I rolled my lips inward and bit down on them, suppressing a smile. There was something mischievous about this man, and I suspected he'd only given me small glimpses of it so far. I wondered what it would be like if he turned his full boyish charm on me. On the exterior, he was a worldly man: rugged and handsome. But inside there was a youthful spirit waiting for any opportunity to come out and play.

The plane shuddered.

Bile rose in my throat, catching me off guard.

I broke out into a cold sweat as nausea overtook me.

Gavin reached down beside his chair and pulled out a small paper bag. "You're pale. Do you need some ginger ale?"

I unfolded the bag and shook my head, too afraid to open my mouth for fear that more than words might come out.

"I'll be right back." Gavin got up and left his seat.

Resting my head back, I took long, slow breaths, hoping to calm the storm churning in my gut.

"Okay, let's get you covered up."

At the sound of Gavin's voice, I opened my eyes, still cautious of making any fast movements. There was an open can of ginger ale on the table in front of me, and he and he was covering me with a blanket.

"Here, lift your head, but do it slowly. Don't make any sudden movements."

He slid a small pillow between me and the seatback, then he sat down and took my free hand in his once again. "There, you might be more comfortable now."

I chanced a quiet "thank you" before shutting my eyes. Keeping them closed made the nausea almost bearable. There was so much we needed to discuss if we were going to convince his family that we were a married couple, but I couldn't think of anything other than my stomach.

Soon after, I must have nodded off. When I woke, the nausea was gone, and I had unconsciously given up the pillow for the comfort of Gavin's shoulder.

"It's about time you joined the land of the living again," he teased, reaching for the aluminum can in front of me. "Drink some ginger ale."

"Thank you. It was sweet of you to make me feel comfortable. I guess it worked a little too well. How long was I out?" I asked before taking a sip of the almost flat soda. It felt good in my dry mouth.

"An hour or so. Have you had a lot of morning sickness?"

His question threw me for a loop. Why was he worried about that? "The plane made me nauseous, not the baby."

He frowned at my reply, adjusting the bookmark in the book he'd been reading. "I'm trying to get to know you better, Ellie. These are things people are going to expect me to know about my pregnant wife. I'd like to answer them with some confidence."

"Oh. No, not really. Today was the worst, but I'm not sure if it was morning sickness or nerves. I was so busy up until now I hadn't thought of it." I peeked over at him and fiddled with the pillow I'd been using. "You know, aside from Ray, you're the only other person I've told." That made the pregnancy feel more real.

He nodded and silence filled the plane as he looked back at the book in his lap. "Gavin, if I'd told you last night, would you have handled my father differently?" Looking down at the pillow I held tight to my chest, I waited for his answer.

"No. If anything, the opposite of that would've been true. The rumors about how hard your life had been were enough to make me fight for you, but if I had known about the..." He paused. "... your baby, I would have been even more determined to make sure you didn't go back with them."

Turning to look at him, I couldn't help but smile. "You were pretty determined as it was. It has to be said. You truly are a good man, Gavin."

"Not always." He winked and I couldn't help but laugh.

I took another sip of ginger ale before setting it back on the table. "Tell me about your family?"

He clicked his tongue. "That isn't fair to you while you're stuck on a plane. You should be free to run away once I tell you about them."

The ominous way he spoke of his family confused me. He was so kind and wonderful. How could his family be any different? I didn't press him any further. He'd extended me the courtesy of dodging some of his questions. It was only fair I did the same for him.

"All right, sleepyhead, we have a lot of ground to cover and not much time. So let's get down to business."

Chapter Six

GAVIN

The Morton ranch sign loomed out in the distance, flanked by two massive redwood logs on either side of the private road that led to the ranch. Ellie gasped and leaned forward, looking up as we passed under the sign.

"Welcome home," I muttered to myself. This was the last thing I had imagined myself doing, and I hadn't had the time to prepare any of them for our arrival. There was no way to know what we were about to walk in to.

"I'm sorry for making you do this, Gavin." Ellie's voice was quiet, and she rested her palm on my leg gently.

I placed my hand over hers and held it tight as we drove deeper into the compound. I pointed to her right. "If you take that road, you'll get to my brother Tyler's house. He lives there with his wife and their son." He smiled. "You'll like Kate. She's a good woman. She whipped my brother into shape. Their son, TJ, is four now."

Ellie craned her neck, catching what glimpse of their house she could between the trees. "Ty and Kate's marriage was arranged by our father and hers. It wasn't good for a while, but they made it work." I guess in a sense their marriage had been fake too, though the circumstances behind it were very different, but now they had the kind of marriage that most people could only dream of.

CHAPTER SIX

A smile crossed my face at the idea of being here to watch my nephew grow. Spending time with him and teaching him some of my old tricks gave me hope that being back home again wouldn't suck the life out of me.

Ellie gasped. No doubt spotting the main house in the distance. I was almost embarrassed by its size. I pointed over at the dash. "My other brother Rob and his wife live in the house across from the big house. Rob was a single dad for a long time. Out of the three of us, he's never strayed far from Mom and Dad. Then Jessica came back, and they rekindled their high school romance. Addie, my niece, is twelve and keeps this family on their toes."

As we closed in on the big house, and I looked over at Ellie. I thought her eyes were going to bug out of her head. I swear I could almost see the wheels turning in her head, and they were about to fall off.

"You grew up here?"

"No, I grew up in Montana. We moved here when I was in high school. My mom's dad had this ranch and left it to her in his will. My parents built this house before we moved here."

I pulled the truck to a stop, and took in my family home, my stomach falling to the floorboards as realization sank in.

Why was I doing this?

I could have put Ellie on a plane and sent her anywhere in the world she wanted to go with enough cash to keep her comfortable while she figured herself out. But no, for some reason, I'm carrying on with this ridiculous scheme and bringing her home to meet my family. I sighed. Something about her being all alone in the world didn't sit right with me. But was I doing right by her bringing her home with me? What she didn't know was that all the money in the world couldn't buy happiness. And though the ranch was pristine in appearance, there was plenty of dirt lurking beneath the surface.

"If you don't want me here, Gavin, we can turn around and leave. Or I'll leave; you can stay. Whatever you think is right." Ellie looked down at her hands.

Coming home had been my decision, and it wasn't right that she was blaming herself for my reservations.

"This is what is best for you right now. Nobody will bother you when they know you're here and with my family." I threaded my fingers through hers and gave her half a smile. "Time to face the music." Wiggling my eyebrows, I tried to break the tension.

Ellie didn't smile as I hoped she would. Instead, she chewed at her lip. The atmosphere between us had gone from light to thick enough to cut with a knife in no time at all. I hopped out of the truck, rounded it, and opened her door. "

As we stepped onto the porch, my mother threw open the door, stepped out, and spread her arms wide, ready to wrap me in a hug. She looked the same: petite, blonde, and immaculate.

"My baby boy has finally come home." She wrapped me up tight and hugged me for what seemed like hours. "You have no idea how happy I am to have you home, Gav." She said in my ear.

"It's good to be here," I muttered.

"Don't lie to your mother. I know this is the last place you want to be." She let me go and patted my cheek. Her smile genuine, but there was concern in her eyes. She knew this place had the potential to crush me. It had proven that time and time again, but I was hoping this time would be different.

"Mom, please meet Ellie Bowers—uh…Ellie Morton. My wife." I turned to look at Ellie, who looked slightly horrified, probably because I'd slipped and used her maiden name. "Sorry," I mouthed.

Her eyes went soft, and her smile returned. She held out her hand for my mom to shake. Her eyes widened, but her smile never wavered. Always cool under pressure. "Oh no, Ellie, we're family now." Mom pulled her into a hug.

Ellie looked at me over mom's shoulder, tears welling in her eyes. Leaving Montana and her family was harder on her than I thought it would be. To me, it was an easy decision. Her father was trying to send her back to a man who'd crushed her.

"Thank you, Mrs. Morton." Ellie said as the women parted.

"Call me Sandra, honey. I can't wait to get to know you better, dear. I was beginning to think we'd never see the day when Gavin would finally settle down. We'd just about given up hope that he'd marry by forty, but here you are. You must be quite something."

Ellie glanced over at me and squinted. What were the chances she hadn't caught on to the married by forty comment? Slim-to-none would be my guess.

"Now come in. The family is waiting to meet you." My mother hooked her arm through Ellie's, leading her into the house as I followed behind.

I had the distinct feeling this wasn't going to be the low-key arrival I was hoping for. "Mom, when you say 'the family,' what do you mean?"

"Everyone, son. We're all happy you're home." She turned over her shoulder and smiled.

"Great." I slowed my steps, falling farther behind the two women. Maybe I could sneak away. I wouldn't have to deal with the looks my brother would give me because I'd almost lost the ranch. Ellie wasn't the only one with secrets. Only, she'd aired her dirty laundry before we said I do. I hadn't found the same courage. She wasn't the only one who stood to benefit from our marriage, but I'd been to chicken to tell her. Running wasn't an option, though. I'd been there and done that before. Besides, it wouldn't be fair to Ellie. I couldn't throw her to the wolves and turn my back, now, could I?

"Look who's finally home." My mother sang out as we walked into the living room.

She was kidding. They were all there, even Nate and Delaney. Mom walked toward Dad, and I stepped next to Ellie, slipping my hand into hers and giving it a squeeze. She held on to mine tightly when she realized the room was full.

"Hey Gavin, welcome home." Tyler came up and gave me a one arm hug followed by a rough pat on the back. "Are you home for good?" He asked in my ear so nobody else could hear.

"Guess we'll see," I answered. I didn't know what else to say.

Even after we'd finished with introductions, eyes were wide. Just like they'd been the other night when I'd caught her off guard in the cabin kitchen.

"Okay, girls, it's time to talk. Let's head to the den." Kate stood and headed out of the room.

"You, too." Jessica leaned across Rob and grabbed Ellie's hand.

Ellie looked at me with a forced smile, so I gave her a reassuring nod. She was in good hands. Me, on the other hand? I was left with my brothers and my father. This might not turn out so well for me. I'd much rather have slipped on a wig and a pair of high heels and joined the women than face the wrath of the Morton men so soon.

Chapter Seven

ELLIE

The den had a wall of windows that overlooked the backyard and beyond. I'd seen quite a few ranches in my time, but this one seemed endless. Miles of land stretched out all around us. So much land that I was beginning to understand how they could afford a private plane and pilot.

The trees were bare, but I could almost imagine this view in the springtime or summer, when each branch was filled with leaves. When the flowers were in bloom, and the birds sang while bees buzzed to and for, finding nectar to bring back to the hive.

There was a long buffet on one wall covered with a spread larger than I had never seen. Ten kinds of cheese, crackers of every shape and size, and more meat than I could have dreamed of. Fruits and veggies as far as the eye could see.

"Welcome to the family, Ellie." Jessica poured a glass of champagne and handed it to me.

"I—I don't drink."

"Sorry, I should have asked first." Jessica took the glass away and poured a glass of juice instead. "Here, try this. We are here to give you all the advice you're going to need. Too bad you can't have the champagne to take the edge off. You're braver than I was. This isn't an easy family to break into. We've all had rough starts, and we wanted to pull you aside because we want you to have a better experience than we did."

CHAPTER SEVEN

Jessica sat in one of the chairs and raised her eyebrows at me while she patted the arm of the one beside her.

Kate sat across from us on the couch. "Tell us all the juicy details. How did you meet Gavin?" She took a sip of her drink and waited for my reply.

Dread rose from the pit of my stomach. Gavin and I hadn't fully discussed what we were going to say. It was only the first question, and I was already being raked over red-hot coals. On the plane, Gavin had told me that the best course of action was to tell enough of the truth that it made sense, but that we should avoid making up too many additional details so we didn't have to remember them all.

"He saved me from a bad situation, and...and well, we just hit it off." I hoped that would do the trick. The women leaned forward, like they were expecting more than I'd offered them.

"And we've been inseparable ever since." I'd left out that it had only been a couple of days.

"Gavin told Tyler that your family didn't approve. Is that right?" Kate questioned.

"That's an understatement if I ever heard one." I didn't mean to speak so off the cuff, but I was tired of my family being the discussion everywhere I went. "I suppose I should say they were surprised at the speed at which Gavin and I moved." That was as close to the truth as I was willing to get for now.

Kate smiled at me warmly. "We were a little surprised also, but I think it's wonderful. Gavin has been lost for a while. I think this marriage is exactly what he needs." Jessica paused on her way to the food table. "Also, this takes care of the caveat that comes along with the ranch. What a load off that was for all of us."

"Caveat? I don't know what you're talking about."

"Oh!" Jessica filled her plate with a few things and hurried back to her seat. "When Tyler was on the brink of turning forty, the boys found out that there was a stipulation in Sandra's father's will. In order for Brian to keep the ranch, the boys all had to be married by the time they were forty."

Kate looked over at Jessica and frowned.

Why wouldn't Gavin have told me about this? It wouldn't have changed anything between us—a fake marriage is a fake marriage, no matter the reasons behind it. In fact, it might have made me feel a bit better had I known he was going to benefit from it. Still, it made me uneasy that he'd kept it from me. He had no reason to. Apparently, he was a closed book about more than just his family.

Jessica opened her mouth like she had more to say, but Kate was glaring at her, although she seemed oblivious to it.

"Do you both work on the ranch?"

Kate smiled and glanced over at Jessica. "I do. Tyler and I own the adjoining ranch. It's my family's ranch." She beamed with pride as she talked.

Jessica shook her head. "I own an event planning company. It keeps me busy, but I help out when I'm needed. Did you work on your ranch? Rob said your family owns property near the Montana ranch."

"They do, but they aren't ranchers. It's set up more like a self-sustaining community. It's complicated. My life back home was complicated." I ducked my head and took a sip of my juice. I hadn't explained most of this to Gavin yet, so I hoped they'd get the hint and drop the subject.

"Complicated is fairly normal around here." Both women laughed, and I smiled, thankful that they didn't press for more details. They were offering their friendship, and they didn't know me. But maybe they were the kind of women I could eventually lean on. Maybe one day I'd open up to them about it all.

Ugh. Fake marriage, Ellie, remember?

It's. A. Fake. Marriage.

Chapter Eight

GAVIN

"She's pretty," my father piped up from his chair.

"Pretty young." Rob chimed as he walked by me. My middle brother always spoke his mind and saw life through a narrow lens. There wasn't room for error in his eyes. He managed Morton Ranch, and his business habits had a tendency to spill over into his personal life. Since they'd gotten married, Jessica had done a world of good for him, but deep down, he was still Rob.

My returned from the kitchen and handed me a drink. "I wasn't aware you were serious with anyone. Not that I mind, but I would have liked to host the wedding. Or at least attend it."

"Thanks mom. The justice of the peace was quick and efficient. Ellie is shy and a big ceremony wasn't really her thing."

"Or yours." My mother replied, arching her brow.

She was right. The last time I had been subjected to a lavish party, my world collapsed. I'd lost my business that night, and since then, I avoided them at all costs.

Dad swirled the ice in his glass. "Is there anything we need to know about this girl?" He leaned forward, resting his elbows on the arm of the chair. His top priority had always been our family's reputation, and he preferred to stay ahead of any issues that could arise.

Oh, you mean, like the identity of her crazy father?

Or his equally insane community of followers?

If not them, maybe her rifle toting pack of brothers…

Then again, there was her ex-fiancé. I hadn't met him, but I was pretty sure he was a huge piece of shit.

And then there was the pregnancy. She was carrying a baby that wasn't mine.

I shook my head. "No. Yes, she's young, and yes, she's pretty. But Ellie is my wife, and she will be treated as such." Standing, I looked pointedly at each of my parents and my brothers, waiting for their smart comments.

My father motioned to the chair. "Gavin, sit down. We're not trying to give you a hard time. We're just happy to have you home. It's been a long time since all you boys were here together."

My brothers nodded in agreement. I wasn't trying to make things difficult, but I wouldn't put up with any backhanded comments from my father. He had a knack for almost destroying lives. He did it to Tyler after he met Kate, and he had made Rob's life pretty miserable when he chased Jessica away all those years ago—although if that hadn't happened, Rob wouldn't have Addie.

My father leaned back in his chair, his eyebrows raised like he was waiting for me to explain. When it was clear, I wasn't going to he continued. "What possessed you to marry this woman without so much as a phone call to your mother and me?"

"She's pregnant."

"Is it yours?" My father's voice dripped with disdain and while I'd like to have smacked the smug look off his face, that wasn't the kind of progress I hoped to make with him on this visit home.

"Yes." I couldn't tell them the truth. They wouldn't understand. Based on the long list of questions and the skeptical looks, they were already worried about how my marriage was going to affect their reputations. "Don't worry, Dad, Ellie's harmless. Our marriage won't do anything that might hurt your precious ranch." I'd had just about enough of the line of questioning for one day, so I stood, excusing myself for my mother's benefit, and left the room.

I hauled our bags in from the truck, placing them in the room that I'd share with Ellie, the one that had always been mine. While I was sure she would have appreciated a room of her own, that would have raised too many eyebrows. I stopped to stare out the window, which overlooked the backyard, feeling like a teen again. I studied the vast space, imagining all the buildings I could fill it with. It was that open space that had made me want to be an architect in the first place. I could still picture what the neighborhood of my design would look like from this vantage point.

The massive window had always been my own makeshift design board. I'd spent many days and nights seated by it sketching out ideas in my various notebooks.

There was a knock on the open door, and I turned just as Rob greeted me with Tyler hot on his heels.

"Might as well come in." As if I had a choice, they'd already welcomed themselves into my space. I turned back, looking at the expanse of the yard. What a waste those years had been. I'd lost my company and the life I'd built for myself. And I was a fool for not predicting it.

I sat on the corner of the king-sized bed. The size could have been considered excessive for a teenage boy, but once the three of us were over six feet, we each got an upgrade.

I didn't really want to hear them out. But I'd already made that clear with my exit, and that hadn't done the trick, so there was no point in trying to get rid of them again. Ever since the gala when my business had tanked, they'd been more like helicopter parents than brothers. Hence the reason I lived in Montana. To get some distance from them, from everything that had happened. That hadn't worked out too well. All I'd managed to do was come home a month early with a wife who was nearly half my age.

Tyler crossed the room and sat down in the chair beside my window. "So, things got a little interesting in Montana."

I rested my elbows on my knees and looked up at him. "You could say that." If I kept my answers short, maybe they'd get bored with this conversation.

Rob joined me on the edge of the bed. "Mom said you introduced Ellie to her as 'Ellie Bowers'. Is Hank Bowers's daughter?"

Nodding, I kept my mouth shut.

"Was this a rescue, Gavin? I know all about Hank Bowers and the 'community' he operates out there. Ellie's what? In her early twenties? That's prime marriage age for that lot." Rob folded his arms across his chest and studied me. He was too perceptive. I wouldn't get away with lying about this.

"Yes, it was." I rubbed a hand over my face. "Look, I don't want mom and dad to know, Ellie has been through enough embarrassment over the entire thing, so please don't say anything. Dad would have a field day with it if he found out."

Tyler leaned forward. "What's the plan, then? How long will this go on for?" He was the practical one of the three of us. If I gave him the chance, he'd think through this situation and figure out all the pitfalls and roadblocks we'd encounter along the way. But I wasn't in the mood to even consider all of that. Ellie and I had done what we'd done, and I had zero regrets, even if I hated all the questions.

"I don't know, until she's safe, I guess."

"Could you make it work? When Kate and I met, we—"

I cut him off. I knew his story. Had seen it play out firsthand, but he was getting way ahead of the situation. "Tyler, I hardly know her. She showed up in my cabin a couple of days ago. I can't imagine we'll live a long and happy life together." Or, at least, I couldn't let myself imagine it. She'd made her intentions clear. This marriage was nothing more than a stepping stone for her.

I flopped back on my bed and stared at the ceiling. Counting the logs used to build the room was something I had done in my youth when I was frustrated, and there I was doing it again. The question was, were my brothers frustrating me or was it the situation with Ellie that had me all twisted?

Rob cleared his throat. "But what about the baby? Once your baby gets here and everyone is attached to the idea of you as a family, there will be no way anyone will let her go."

I hung my head before I admitted the truth. "The baby isn't mine." I didn't look at either brother, but I could imagine the shock on their faces.

"Gavin?" They said at the same time.

My old chair creaked as Tyler shifted his weight in it. "You're really risking everything, aren't you?"

Sitting up, I looked at Tyler, then Rob. "Look, I don't know what the plan is. Does there have to be one? This is me. This is who I am. I'm the brother who doesn't think about the consequences. Who doesn't care what will happen at the end of the day? Did you expect anything less? Judging by your relentless questioning of the entire situation, you didn't. Congratulations, you've sussed me out. Happy now?" I waited for a comeback, but none came.

Tyler stood and moved closer. "Sounds like you've thought of everything and nothing all at the same time." He patted my shoulder. "We only want what's best for you, and maybe you might not see it yet, but Ellie could be exactly who you need." He left the room.

"This isn't just some further crisis as a result of the past year, is it?" Rob asked, looking at the floor.

It was the question on everyone's mind, I'm sure. Had losing everything I'd built caused me to cling to Ellie in some pathetic attempt to add value to my shattered life? "No Rob, it's really not. I'm over what happened. Am I happy my business went down in flames because of my business partner? No, but it's given me some time to reevaluate my goals and what I want to do from here."

"Care to share?"

"Not right now, but soon. It might involve me coming back here. Hope that's all right with everyone."

"I don't think anyone will mind." Rob patted my leg and got up to leave. "You may want to rescue your bride. She's been with the girls for a while."

Smiling, I stood and followed him out. "I'm sure she's had quite the education on this family."

But there was more to it than that. Even though we'd only been separated for a short while, I missed my wife.

Chapter Nine

ELLIE

Gavin stepped into the den and headed straight for me. "I hope you haven't told my wife all the family dirt just yet." He was followed by his brother, Rob.

They were both strong, handsome men, but Gavin's beard had grown scruffy over the past couple of days, and he had hair—dark and shiny and just a little too long—that any woman would want to run her hands through. Would I ever get to experience that firsthand? Although I wanted to deny it, I secretly hoped so. He was nothing like Ray, thank God, and asking for anything more seemed out of the realm of possibility, but it couldn't stop it from crossing my mind every now and again.

Gavin was tall and broad. He made me feel safe. Ray was shorter than me, and though the two men were probably around the same age, he wasn't as well maintained as Gavin was. His balding head and beady eyes didn't illicit any response in me. But the man I was looking up at now? That was a different story?

"Can I steal my bride away?" Gavin rested his hand on my shoulder and ran his thumb along my neck, eliciting a shiver from me.

It's all a show, Ellie.

Ellie? He even had me calling myself by the nickname now.

Regardless, he was putting on a performance for his family and when we were alone, he would, no doubt, drop the act and go back to his regular self. Not that he was a bad guy at all, but we would fall back into our reality when we didn't have an audience.

He'd married me to get me away from my family, except maybe that wasn't the only reason. But why hadn't he told me he needed to be married by forty? It seemed like an important detail to leave out. But if anything, it only confirmed that this was temporary. I'd told him my secrets, and he hadn't let me in at all.

"We should get unpacked before supper, and I could use a quick shower." I stood and set my plate on the table. "Thank you all for the wonderful welcome. I truly appreciated it." Sliding my hand into Gavin's, I let him lead me out of the room.

Thankfully, the stairs were just outside the den entrance, so we were able to escape any other prying eyes quickly.

Gavin closed the door behind us, and I flopped down on the bed and stared at the ceiling fan.

"I don't think I've ever been so nervous in my life—no, that's not true. The night my father showed up is right up there with this." When he didn't respond, I turned my head and found him staring out the window into the damp, gray day.

Something felt different between us in that moment. Even if I was his wife on paper only, he'd done so much for me in such a short amount of time. In return, I hoped I could keep him happy.

"Penny for your thoughts?" I murmured. He probably wouldn't open up, but I had to try.

"I don't even know what I'm thinking." He turned from the window and looked at me, his brow furrowed, and his nose scrunched. "My father asked if you had any skeletons, so I told everyone about the baby."

My heart raced in my chest. They knew? What did they think? Would they talk Gavin out of our arrangement?

"They all think it's mine. Don't worry." He came closer, his facial expression softening, and placed a hand on my cheek.

I soaked in the heat from his palm. He'd lied to his family, and for some crazy reason, that put me at ease when it should have had me panicking. It was one thing to pretend we were married, but he may have gone too far by getting their hopes up about the baby. I'd only just met them, but the idea of telling them the baby wasn't Gavin's, then walking away seemed cruel.

Knowing I was in the early stages of my first trimester, I'd figured I could get out of Dodge before started showing and his family would be none the wiser, but he'd gone ahead and spoiled that plan. Still, there was something about this man that his family didn't understand. As much as he could set my body on fire with a glance, he could also put my mind at ease with about the same amount of effort. The more time I spent with him, the more I saw past the tough exterior he'd constructed for himself to deal with whatever life threw his way. As our time together went on, I got more and more glimpses of the little boy who wanted to be loved for who he was.

"Maybe we shouldn't have come. I can go back to Montana. I'll deal with whatever consequences come my way. I don't want you to face any more wrath for making the mistake of marrying me."

"You aren't leaving. I will never send you back to those people." He moved his hand off my cheek and pulled me into a hug. "What you and I did isn't normal, but I wouldn't call it a mistake. As long as I have a say, you're staying right here with me, understood?"

I searched his eyes. Was he serious? Or was he making a joke that I didn't understand? Why did he care so much about me? I was a virtual stranger.

But in his eyes, I found nothing but fierce honesty.

I stepped back from him. "I need to clean up. Where's the bathroom?"

He pointed at the wooden door I'd thought was a closet. "The en suite bathroom is through there."

I shook my head and huffed out a laugh.

Of course, he had an en suite. It would take time to get used to living in this kind of luxury, but maybe it was for the best if I didn't allow myself to get too comfortable. Not when we both knew it would eventually come to an end.

Chapter Ten

GAVIN

Ellie went into the bathroom with a change of clothes, but instead of turning on the shower like I expected, she ran a bath, and the sound of the water filling the jacuzzi tub made me smile. A soak in the tub would be the perfect way for her to relax after a long day of travel and what had been a rather uneventful meeting with my family. She may not have had it as bad as I did, but her nerves were probably shot after the events of the past couple of days and having to deal with my family on top of the stress she'd already been carrying.

There was something about her that made me want to put her needs before my own. I'd inadvertently opened myself up to a need to protect her no matter what or who we were up against, and that wasn't a feeling I was used to.

Splash.

Thump.

I hopped up from the bed and raced to the bathroom door. The noise had come from inside. "Are you all right in there?"

"Uh, yeah, I just..."

I placed my palm flat against the door. "You just what?"

No reply.

"Ellie?"

I rapped on the door. She still didn't answer.

"Are you okay?"

No answer again.

I tried the knob. It was locked. Of course it was.

Damn it.

Something was wrong. I could feel it in my gut. I took a few steps back and kicked at the door. It flew inward with ease and slammed against the wall. Inside, in the middle of the floor was Ellie, naked and curled into a ball. A pool of water surrounded her body. I ripped an oversized towel from the rack and hurried to her side, covering her with it before shaking her shoulder. She didn't stir, so I scooped her up off the floor, her long fiery hair soaking the sleeve of my shirt in an instant. Her body curled against mine as I carried her to the bedroom.

She came to in my arms, startled to find herself naked and pressed against my chest, I was sure. Her firm, perky breasts were on full display.

All of her was.

I tried my best not to gawk. She was awake, and that was progress, but was she ill? Had she slipped? I set her down on the bed and pulled the blanket over her naked body concealing her and tucking the edges. Only her head poked out of the cocoon I'd encased her in.

"Are you okay?"

She nodded. "I must've run the bath too hot," she panted out.

If she was too hot, maybe I shouldn't have wrapped her in a blanket.

Hell, I didn't know what I was doing.

"Water, please."

Of course. I raced back into the bathroom, skidding through the pool of water on the floor, but I latched on to the counter and kept myself upright.

Calm down, Gavin.

I wouldn't be any good to her if I didn't. I grabbed the cup from the counter, rinsed it, and filled it with the coldest water the tap could manage. Then I made my way back to her, careful of the water on the floor this time around.

She pushed herself up to take the glass from me, and in the process, the blanket inched down, revealing the top of her breasts. My eyes instinctively dropped, but I forced myself to look back up. To distract myself, I pulled the soaked strands of her hair that clung to her all too beautiful face while she eyed me over the rim of the glass as she drank from it.

She set the empty glass on the bedside table.

"Want some more."

She shook her head. "No, thanks, I'm feeling much better now. I just ran the bath the same temperature as I always do."

I huffed out a laugh. "Knowing women, it was almost hot enough to boil you alive."

She quirked a half smile. "Almost. Anyhow, my tolerance must be down. Maybe because of the pregnancy? I got woozy, and as I was trying to get a drink from the sink, I got hit by a major dizzy spell. And then, judging by the fact that you carried me to bed, I passed out."

Was that normal? I didn't have enough experience around pregnant women to know whether it was. "Have you been to see a doctor yet?"

"No, not yet. I didn't want word getting around about the baby. You never know who you're going to run into in a small town. If you're doing something you don't want people knowing about, it's almost a guarantee that you're going to get caught."

"I'll ask Kate and see if you can get in with her doctor. She knows more about all of this than I do."

"Oh, you're not a pregnancy expert?" she said, trying to keep a straight face.

I patted my abs. "Nope. It's been years since I last gave birth. I couldn't maintain this washboard stomach if I kept popping out babies, now, could I?"

"Washboard? Really, Gavin?" She rolled her eyes at me.

Seeing her humor return was a relief. She had really scared me earlier.

"You wouldn't be questioning it if you'd had the privilege of seeing my naked body. I'll show you."

"No, no. I believe you." She waved her hand in my direction.

"You don't want to see my bare chest?"

"It's not that. I do—I mean—I don't even know what I want anymore."

I sighed. "It's only fair. You showed me yours."

She laughed. "While naked and passed out on the floor."

"Still counts. I was this close—" I held my finger and thumb up with a tiny gap between them. "—to giving them mouth-to...tit resuscitation." Even I couldn't keep a straight face with that one. I grabbed my shirt and popped it open. One of the snaps decided to jump on the bandwagon and flew across the room and rolled under the chair.

My buttons weren't the only thing popping, though. Ellie's eyes were as wide as ever as she stared at my chest. Washboard or not, her expression told me she was impressed.

She perused my body, taking in every inch of bare skin I'd put on display, until she met my gaze. I couldn't take it anymore. I leaned over her on the bed, my arms on either side of her, caging her in, my face only inches from hers. My mouth centimeters from her soft, kissable lips.

"Ellie." I kept my voice low. "Give me permission to touch you this once, and I promise you won't regret it."

She shook her head.

Damn. I thought I had her. I fell back, resigned for the moment. "Can't say I didn't try."

"We need to talk."

Chapter Eleven

ELLIE

A cold sweat broke out across my brow. Confrontation and I were not friends. It was the reason I'd run from my family instead of standing up for myself.

"I know you had to get married before you turned forty, or you would cost your family the ranch." Crossing my arms over my chest allowed me a little extra space from his body. The smooth skin of chest was distracting, and I needed the distance to have this conversation.

"Who told you that?" He spat.

"Kate." My resolve for this battle was waning. But I thought back to the revelation from my sister-in-law. He hadn't trusted me with this bit of information, and that made me wonder what else he was holding back. I wanted him. I really did. It had taken every ounce of self-control I had to turn down his advance. But I knew that if we were going to cross that divide, we had to get to know one another. It would be too easy for us to get caught if we didn't flush out the details and be completely transparent with each other.

I had bared my soul to Gavin, and I'd told him the absolute truth before I let him marry me, but the same couldn't be said for him, and it hurt. He had every opportunity to mention it, but he'd chosen to let me marry him, unaware of the implications.

"She needs to learn to keep her mouth shut. What else did she tell you?" Gavin took a step back from me.

I'd expected his response to be something along the lines of "I wanted to tell you, but I didn't know how," not the hostility that was emanating from him now.

"Nothing," I looked at my hands, clasped tightly in my lap.

"Well, now you know. Don't read too much into it. No matter what, I wouldn't have let Adam take the ranch. Yes, you solved the problem, but it's not something you need to concern yourself with."

"What were you going to do? Buy him out? Rumor around the mountain has it you most of your money from the business is gone or tied up in legal fees from the embezzlement charges." I lifted my eyebrows, feeling brave. I might not have walked into this marriage with all the knowledge I had now, but I was going to make him talk to me.

One couldn't always trust the gossip heard around the mountain, but I was his wife now, and I needed the truth so I'd be equipped to handle any questions I might encounter

"You know nothing about me or my situation, Elyse."

"That's the point. I'm trying to get to know you better. I've told you everything, and I expected the same from you."

"No, you've told me only what benefits your situation. What benefit is there for me if I open up to you about mine? We've known each other two days. Two days. It's my family that stands to lose out if things go south. I'm sorry if me mitigating damage means I'm not emotionally fulfilling whatever little fantasy scenario you're imagining exists between us."

"Imagining? I'm imagining it? You just tried to seduce me, Gavin."

He ran his hand through his hair and huffed. "Look, I know you've been sheltered your whole life, but in my world—he real world—sex is just that. Sex. Sometimes it means something more, and other times, it doesn't."

I hadn't been imagining the way he looked at me. I was sure of it. Downstairs he had to pretend, but up here, the way he looked at me was real. "So, which is it this time?"

He opened his mouth to reply, only to be interrupted by a knock followed by Sandra's voice through the door. "Gavin, honey, I need a hand downstairs."

Gavin stood from the bed. "Supper will be ready soon. Make yourself presentable." He turned and left the room, clicking the door closed behind him.

I didn't want to move from the bed. His words left me feeling stripped bare. My nose stung, signally the tears that would soon fall, and I didn't want Gavin to see me when they did. He'd made me feel small and silly, and the last thing I needed was for him to see me in this moment of weakness. The tears welling in my eyes may have been about him, but if our conversation was any indication, they weren't for him. I walked to the bathroom, stopping to run my fingers over the splintered door frame before I entered the room and took a seat on the edge of the tub and studied the floor where I'd been lying when Gavin picked me up and cradled me in his arms.

His hands had been gentle and caring when he'd bundled me in the blanket. His face had shown concern for the baby. For one brief moment, it had felt like we were really a family. How could he imply that none of that meant anything? I might have been naive, but I wasn't stupid. I knew well enough to know when a guy was looking at me some kind of way. But maybe he'd done us a favor. He was keeping his boundaries in place in this fake marriage, and I needed to do the same.

The decision was necessary but left feeling isolated. Wrapping my arms around myself, I finally let the tears fall. They weren't just for Gavin. They were for the life I hadn't taken the time to grieve, the life I left behind. Maybe it would have been easier to live as a shunned woman. At least I would have been at home where life was familiar. I could have found friends and a place to live not far from where I'd grown up. But I could do that here too. I just had to stop myself from getting too caught up in Gavin's world and the fantasy that it might someday be mine too.

In the meantime, I needed to make myself presentable and continue the charade Gavin and I had created. I stood and looked in the mirror before I turned the water on and washed my face, applied makeup, and dressed.

Holding my head high, I walked out of the room and downstairs, following the sound of chatter to the den.

If there was one thing life in the community had taught me, it was how to put on an act. I pasted a smile on my face and crossed the room to where Gavin sat and kissed him on the cheek. "Thank you for letting me rest. I feel so much better."

"I'm glad you feel better," he muttered, a look of confusion crossing his face before he could stop it, then he placed a chaste kiss on my lips. It might have shocked me if appearances hadn't been paramount in the Morton family.

Brian, Gavin's dad, cleared his throat, and I turned to see the whole room had turned their attention to us.

Gavin stepped back wearing an unreadable expression—did I see apology in his eyes?—then he bent forward and whispered in my ear. "Are you all right?"

I painted on the fake smile I'd mastered years ago. "Perfect."

It may not have been true in the moment, but it would be. I was getting exactly what I'd asked for from the outset. Placing my hand over my belly I took a deep breath. We'd found our way out. I just needed to stay strong and keep focused for the baby. No more distractions.

Chapter Twelve

Ellie

The days turned to weeks, and I was settling in to life here on the Morton ranch.

Gavin and I didn't stick around too long most nights after supper. We had usually seen very little of each other during the day, so we used this time to portray a happy newly married couple. He didn't have a typical bedroom. His room was more like a suite and was attached to a well-stocked library. I likened it to chateaus or villas I had seen in magazines. There had been nothing like this where I grew up. Homes were run down and, in some cases, falling down. But the Morton main house looked like a castle in comparison.

Tonight, when I stepped inside the room, I went to the far end, where his library was.

Two chairs flanked the large window that overlooked a pasture. Large wooden bookshelves lined the wall from floor to ceiling. A library ladder stood along each side of the shelves that slid along tracks for easy access to the books on the top shelves. If Heaven was a library with overstuffed chairs, I was definitely there.

Sitting in one chair, I caught sight of papers sitting on the table.

"Well, what do you think?" Gavin spoke as he sat down in the chair across from me.

I hadn't heard him come in. "What is all this?" I asked, picking up the top page. "Are you starting a new business?" He nodded.

He nodded. "I did some research in Montana, and I asked my business analyst to apply the metrics here."

"And?" I asked rather impatiently.

"It's a more profitable idea here than I ever imagined. What I'm going to do is build state-of-the-art architectural homes. They'll be built to specifications on site, then moved in pieces to their forever locations." He looked at the papers I had placed back on the table before he crossed his arms behind his head and stretched his long legs out. The stubble on his face made him look distinguished and made my heart flutter a little. The men in the community were required to be clean shaven, so to me, men with five o'clock shadows had always been mysterious and sexy.

"Ellie, are you listening?" His question shook me back to reality.

"Umm, no, sorry. I was lost in another thought?" I stammered.

"One related to the business?" he asked.

"Well, kind of," I mumbled. It wasn't an outright lie. "You're talking about ready to move homes that aren't the typical style?" The plans here were stunning. "I know you can't build every style of home you're going to offer but will you use an example home furnished with the different finishes you are going to offer? That way you can show how it will be moved and things like that." When Gavin didn't respond, I looked up from the plans.

He had a pen in hand and was writing frantically. "What else you got?" he asked, an eager expression on his face.

"What about packages? Like gold, silver, and bronze? Each gets a different level of personalized interaction. Bronze, for those who choose to do the consults over video conference rather than in person. That way, your market can extend outside of Texas. Silver, they come to the site and walk through the sample home and pick their finishes. Gold, flown in on the jet, put up at a hotel in Dallas and brought here by a car service. Really wine and dine them." I shrugged. It was basic and maybe small-minded, but Gavin ate it up like it was the best thing he had ever heard.

"What should your title be?" He raised one eyebrow at me.

"You want my help?" I hedged.

"Well, yes. You're my wife. For however long you want to be. We should work together too." He said without hesitation.

"I have no education Gavin, so I doubt I'll be much help. I don't even know how to run the simplest things on a computer."

Leaning over, he placed his hand on my knee. "We'll get you training for anything you want to do. Right now, I'm just happy you're as excited as I am about this. Don't tell anyone yet. I am just checking into the viability right now." His words were firm, but he didn't have to say them to me. This was his news not mine so it wouldn't come from my lips.

"I won't say a word. But you will keep me updated, right?" I asked, hoping he wouldn't leave me out.

He stood and moved over to the television and turned it on before flopping down on the bed.

This has become our nightly routine. We would talk some. Then he would watch TV, and I would read. But tonight, I wanted to be closer to him. I could still feel his hand on my knee, and I wanted to feel more.

I settled in next to him, and he turned to look at me. "Well, this is a nice surprise." He held out his arm, and I scooted closer, snuggling up against his side.

My heart was racing. We had been this close multiple times, but tonight was different. Was it because he had opened up about the business? Or was it because he believed in me and wanted my opinion and help?

"Ellie," Gavin whispered. "I want to kiss you."

"I wouldn't put up a fight," I replied, giving him a soft smile.

He lowered his head and brushed his mouth against mine. If I thought my pulse had been racing before, it was as if I had been running a marathon now. Gavin's lips were soft, but his kiss was forceful, passionate, and possessive. Our tongues fought for space.

The show on the television long forgotten, Gavin rolled over so his body pressed against mine. Breaking the kiss, he looked at me, breathing heavy, just like I was. "Well, that's not where I thought this would go," he said as he smiled sheepishly.

"I thought it was nice," I replied quietly, looking away from his eyes.

"Look at me, Ellie."

When I obeyed, he continued. "Do not ever be ashamed of how you feel."

His words made me think back to all the times Ray had made me feel dirty after sex.

"Besides, we're married." He claimed my lips again, and I wrapped my arms around him. He was an amazing kisser, and the feelings coursing through my body were different from anything I had experienced before.

Was this what falling in love felt like?

Chapter Thirteen

Ellie

I couldn't believe how fast time passed here. Back in Montana, it dragged, and every day felt like it was four days long, but here, I was just over halfway through my pregnancy. Kate pulled up to the house in her SUV, and I let out a sigh of relief. Gavin had been threatening to come with me all week. Kate and I had decided she would come to my OB appointments with me because Gavin couldn't get away from the ranch. I didn't mind. I'd looked forward to our days together—I'd never really had girlfriends—so Gavin wanting to intrude was less than exciting.

When I climbed in, she was grinning from ear to ear. "Are you excited to find out if it's a boy or girl?"

"I am. Part of me doesn't want to know, but the other part of me needs to plan for this little one." I grinned and buckled my seatbelt before Kate backed out of the driveway and headed down the driveway.

"That's odd," Kate muttered as she slowed to a stop between the main house and Rob's home.

"What's wrong?" I asked.

"Feels like something is wrong with a tire. Let me look."

"I can check this side," I said as I reached for the buckle on the seatbelt.

"No." Kate all but shouted. "It will only take me a second." She hopped out of the vehicle, but she took her purse...

As I turned and watched for her to come around my side to look at the tires, the door slammed, and the SUV shifted into gear. I turned in my seat, wondering why she hadn't checked the passenger side, and came face to face with my husband.

"What are you doing?" I looked out the window for Kate, but she was running through the side door of the big house.

"I'm taking you to this appointment and every one from here on out." He stepped on the accelerator and headed for the doctor's office. "Look, I know I haven't been there for you, and I'm the one that should have been at these appointments. Nothing here was more important than making sure you and the baby are healthy, but I'm here now, and I am not going anywhere." Turning onto the highway, he held his hand out palm up for me to take.

His hand was warm on my thigh, and I couldn't help placing mine on top of it. "Forgive me for not making these appointments a priority?"

"I forgive you." My words were quiet, and I wasn't sure I meant them.

"You don't sound overly enthused that I want to be there."

"Gavin, it's not that. I know you're busy on the ranch and it changes more than just your day to come with me." I shrugged and looked out the window.

"So, you're worried about the ranch running smoothly?"

"No." I huffed.

"Ellie, I want to be there for you and this baby. Things aren't normal, I get it but you deserve all the support I can give you." His hand tightened around mine.

"Okay. We'll do this together." I smiled softly at him and breathed a sigh of relief.

The rest of the drive was quiet, and I was a bundle of nerves walking into the clinic. The anatomy scan was worrying me, and Gavin couldn't sit still. "Would you quit bouncing around? You're making me seasick, and we're hours from the ocean."

"I'm excited. Sue me."

"Ellie Morton," the nurse called from the desk. All eyes turned to us as we stood and followed the woman down the hall.

"Right in there. Unbutton your pants and slide them below your hips. Hop up on the bed, and the tech will be right with you," she said. She'd barely made it inside the room before she turned around and left, closing the door behind her.

I stared at Gavin, the chaos of our delivery to the ultrasound room ratcheting up my anxiety.

"Well, I guess I could do the honors if you want," he teased as he reached for me "This isn't exactly where I thought I would finally get you out of your pants, but I won't complain."

Slapping his hand away from the button of my jeans, I shook my head. His eyes were dancing, and despite the stress of the day, his mischievous ways had me wanting to burst out laughing.

Lying back on the exam table, I pulled the blanket up to cover myself, but Gavin pulled it down to expose my swollen abdomen. He placed his hand on it and grinned. It was the first time he had done this. The light pressure from his hand sent tingles through my body. Something had changed in him, and I wasn't going to complain.

"All right, Ellie, let's get a look at this little one." The tech came in and stopped in her tracks. "Oh, hi. I thought Kate would be here with Ellie."

"I'm Gavin. The dad." He beamed and looked over at me.

"Well, this is exciting. Let's get started." The tech sat beside the bed and squirted the warm jelly on my stomach.

She moved the probe around and clicked the mouse as she measured. "Look up at that screen, and we'll see whether your little person is a boy or a girl." Her warm smile settled my nerves, and I turned my attention to the screen at the foot of the bed.

"Is that the baby?" Gavin whispered.

I nodded, watching a look of awe spread across his face.

"Wow. That's amazing." He turned his attention back to the screen.

After several minutes and lots of pushing on my abdomen, the tech huffed a sigh. "Looks like the Morton stubbornness has been passed on to this little one. I can't tell you with any certainty whether it's a boy or girl. I'm so sorry." She clicked off the screen and handed Gavin the pictures.

"Do you have another ultrasound scheduled after this?" he asked, looking at the printout in his hands.

"No, not unless there are any complications." She smiled, but Gavin's face fell a little.

"Thank you," I said, hoping to list the mood, and sat up.

She nodded and walked out of the room.

"Well, this sucks. Maybe we can schedule another one. We can pay a private clinic." Gavin ran his hand through his hair while he looked at the ultrasound photos.

"It's okay. In a few months, we will know. Finding out now won't change the outcome." I walked over to him and took the pictures out of his hand. "This little person is going to be amazing." The black and white images barely resembled a baby, but as I studied them, I fell more in love with our child.

I handed the photos back to him and buttoned my jeans, then laced my arm through his. "Now, it is tradition after appointments that we get milkshakes and chicken wings. You up for it?"

Gavin pulled open the door, and we walked out of the room. "I won't argue that one. When we get home, I might try to get you out of those jeans again." He winked, and I couldn't help but laugh.

Chapter Fourteen

ELLIE

The Christmas tree stood tall in the center of the room. It was impeccably decorated, and there were presents piled high in front of it. Gavin and I had been taking things fairly slow, but since the ultrasound, he'd been nothing short of attentive. It was tough to turn down his many advances, but I'd managed to keep things friendly aside from the odd surprise kiss that lasted too long. I wanted to get to know him before we jumped into bed together. But even I was getting tired of how slow things were progressing between us physically. There was nothing to blame Gavin for. It was me and my own insecurities holding me back, but now it was time to take the next step and I had a plan.

The chatter in the living room was refreshing. I'd spent so many years wondering what a real family Christmas would be like, and here I was in the middle of one.

Grabbing my phone, I sent a text to Gavin.

Me: Thank you for giving me a real Christmas.

Gavin: You've never had a Christmas?

Me: Nope. My family never celebrated it.

Gavin: I am happy you're here with me.

I looked up and peered around the tree. Our eyes met, and I smiled at him.

Me: Merry Christmas, husband.

Taking a deep breath, I attached three pictures for him and waited for his reaction.

Gavin picked up his phone from the armrest of the couch again. A frown crossed his face when he saw the text. Then I watched him turn so Tyler, who was sitting beside him, couldn't see while he scrolled through the pictures, his brow furrowed. He set his phone back down before he picked it up again and scrolled once more. I watched as the frown changed to a slight smile at his second inspection. He cleared his throat and scratched his chin, then he looked up at me and shook his head. The smile turning into a grin.

I bobbled my phone at the shot of joy I felt when he looked at me. I grabbed it before it could fall, and when I looked back to where Gavin had been sitting, he was gone. The room was large, but he was nowhere to be seen.

"Come with me." His warm breath on the back of my neck made me jump. His voice was stern, the complete opposite of what I expected after the look he'd just given me, but I did what he said.

He was walking so quickly tjat I had to almost run to keep up with him. Taking the stairs two at a time, he reached the second floor when I was about halfway up the stairs.

"Gavin, what's wrong? I'm sorry—I shouldn't have sent those." I sprinted into our bedroom behind him.

Gavin closed the door the second I entered the room. The click of the lock would forever be a sound I remembered.

He stepped toward me. "You should be sorry."

"I am. Let's just go down back downstairs and forget it ever happened. I didn't mean to ruin Christmas."

He shook his head, his expression serious, his eyes boring into me. "The only thing you have to be sorry about is not sending them sooner. And we're not going anywhere until I get to unwrap my Christmas present."

I sucked in a breath. He wasn't mad?

"Take off your clothes."

"Right now? Gavin, it's daylight out, and your family is downstairs."

"Elyse, take off your clothes. You can't send me pictures like that if you aren't going to follow through." He moved closer to me and reached for the hem of my shirt. "If you won't remove your clothes, I'll do it for you."

Gavin slid my shirt up and over my head, then tossed it over his shoulder. "Is this what you want, Ellie?" He traced the curve along the top of my breast.

A shiver ran through me at his touch. "I wouldn't have sent those photos to you if I didn't want it to end this way." I reached behind me and unclasped my bra and let it fall to the floor.

Gavin's eyes were glued to my breasts. "I can't believe how much fuller they are than the last time I saw them. God, Ellie, you are gorgeous."

He closed the distance between us and wrapped his arms around me. Kissing me with unbridled hunger, and he didn't stop until he had me breathless and weak in the knees. He kissed down my neck and along my collarbone, taking one breast in his hand and kneading it.

He reached down between us and popped the button of my jeans open. "Take your pants off."

I obeyed his command. It was a side of Gavin I didn't know existed. He had been so sweet, patient, and gentle with me any time he'd touched me. Always careful to ask permission. But that was out the window now. I'd given him the permission he'd long wanted, and this was what was on the other side of that.

I slid my jeans down my hips, and they fell the rest of the way to the floor with a light thud, and he took a step back and scanned my body. He lingered on my stomach, rounder than the last time he'd seen it. Even though most days I felt less than sexy, Gavin couldn't seem to keep his eyes off me.

He lifted me, and I wrapped my legs around his hips as he carried me to the bed we'd been sharing for weeks. We'd only truly come close to doing this once before, and I'd turned him away because I wasn't ready. He placed me on the bed and kissed me before he stood up.

Without taking his eyes off me, he pulled his shirt out of the waist of his pants and unbuttoned it slowly. "Are you sure this is what you want?" His voice was low and full of lust. Lust that was all for me. There was nobody else in the world I wanted to share this moment with.

"I do. I want you, Gavin."

His jeans hit the floor, and his belt buckle landed with a clank. He had told me of his life wearing suits, but I couldn't see it. The plaid shirts and the Wranglers seemed like they'd been created exclusively for him.

The bed shifted under the weight, and he slid his hand across my tender nipples, teasing them. I inhaled sharply as he lightly pinched and toyed with my taut buds. I was so aroused, I barely knew what to do with myself. The sensation was intoxicating and overwhelming at the same time. I moaned to relieve some of the tension.

"You have no idea how long I've waited to hear you do that." His words were spoken in hushed tones as he nuzzled his face into my neck, sucking on my earlobe.

"They're so sensitive right now. I read that will happen for the first few months." Why was I talking? He didn't need to know the ins and outs of pregnancy while we were naked in bed together for the first time. At least I was naked; he still wore his underwear.

"I know. I've been reading too."

"You have?"

He stopped his exploration of my breasts and propped himself up on his elbow.

"Of course. You and I are in this together. I'll be here for you and this baby no matter what happens between us." He leaned down and sealed his promise with a kiss.

Gavin moved his hand from my breast and slid it down between my legs. In the few times I had been with Ray, I had never been touched so tenderly. Like my needs mattered. I let my legs open so he had easier access.

"My, my. You are more than ready for me, aren't you?"

He slipped out of his boxers, his cock springing free.

I sucked in a breath at the sight of him. "I could say the same about you, husband."

I leaned over and took his erection in my hand and pumped it a few times. I had never been so bold in my life. What was it about Gavin that made me feel like I could do anything?

He let me explore him for a moment longer, then he positioned himself between my legs, and I braced myself for the pain that was to come.

Chapter Fifteen

GAVIN

Something changed. I'd lowered myself toward Ellie, and she'd tensed up. I pulled back and tucked a strand of hair behind her ear while I studied her face for any clue as to what had caused her reaction. The last thing I wanted to do was overwhelm her. "I'll be gentle, baby."

She nodded, relaxing a bit.

"Are you sure you want to do this?" I asked. I didn't want her to think she couldn't stop things now.

She nodded again, this time adding a quiet "yes" and a small smile. She gripped my hips and pulled me closer, so I complied.

I took care as I entered her for the first time, easing in a bit before pulling back out, then moving inside her a bit more.

Her body welcomed me, a warm blanket wrapped snugly around my cock. I held still, relishing in the feel of her while letting her adjust to my size. After a few moments, I pulled out almost all the way and plunged back inside. Ellie moaned in response, and when I was confident it was a sound of passion and not pain, I continued. This woman deserved every ounce of pleasure I intended to give her.

I may have joked about her being my Christmas present, but my intent was to do most of the giving. I wanted to show her exactly what sex should be. How good it could feel. And judging by her response, I was succeeding. She raked her fingers over my back, her fiery hair flowing over the pillow a stunning image I wanted to memorize. My heart had been closed off from love for the past year. Naomi was the woman I thought I was going to spend the rest of my life with, but she decided she didn't want long distance anymore, and I wasn't ready to walk away from my architecture business. We parted ways, and I had regretted it for most of this year.

There had been a few one-night stands, but they were nothing. When I looked at Ellie, I felt the cracks appearing. They had been since the moment I met her. She was kind and pure and good.

Her moan brought me back to reality. Plunging back into her warm core, I did my best to make her scream my name.

She wrapped her legs around me and cried out. "Gavin, please. Oh, Gavin. I have to." She was panting, her body tightening around me. Grabbing her tit, I played with her nipple while I maintained my punishing rhythm.

"Oh god, Gavin. Gavin." Spasms rocked her body, and I couldn't hold back my release. I exploded inside her but continued to move, drawing out her orgasm. When it subsided, I collapsed on top of her, grinning at the soft sigh she made.

"Merry Christmas, Ellie," I whispered as I rolled off and gathered her in my arms.

She rested her head on my chest and ran her hand over my chest. "Can I ask you something?"

"Ask me anything," I replied, letting my eyes flutter shut.

"Is it always like that?" Her words were quiet and unsure.

My eyes flew open, and I stared at the ceiling for a moment before I responded. "What do you mean?"

"Sex, is it supposed to be like that all the time?" Her voice was hesitant but also filled with curiosity.

"What has it been like for you?" I wrapped my arms around her to give her comfort as I asked what might be an uncomfortable question.

"You were so caring, so attentive to me. It's never been like that before. He never worried about me, only that he was satisfied." She sniffled, and a tear dropped to my chest.

"I'm so sorry, baby. I can't tell you what others are like when they make love, but I promise you right now that any time you and I are together, it'll be my mission to make sure you are satisfied."

I'd never envisioned myself with a wife or a family. Now here I was, making assurances and playing house with the most wonderful woman I could have imagined. I wasn't the father of her baby, but no one would know that but us, and over the past few weeks, I'd found myself I'd been imagining what it would be like to be that baby's father. What it would be like to make Ellie and the baby permanent in my life.

Ellie deserved better than what her past life had offered her, but she also deserved better than me. A man who'd lost everything he'd worked toward. Sure, I had aspirations for the future, but I hadn't made any moves. I looked down at her taking comfort in how peaceful she looked, her eyes closed and her lips parted. I kissed her on the forehead and chuckled. I thought men were the ones who passed out after sex. I closed my eyes, figuring I might as well join her.

A pounding on the door woke me from a peaceful dream. "Gavin, get out of bed. It's time to eat, and mom said if you aren't down in five, she's coming in." Rob hollered from the other side of the door.

"What time is it?" Ellie sat straight up and wrapped the sheet around her.

I wanted to laugh at how adorable she was, but I didn't want to embarrass her. We'd achieved a level of intimacy she had been taught was reserved for married couples. I'd seen every part of her. Touched her bare flesh and made her scream my name while I was buried deep inside her. In time, she'd realize the sheet wasn't necessary.

"It's six. Shit, we've been up here since three." Flinging the blankets off, I stood up and searched the floor for my clothes. "Be right down," I called out to Rob.

He didn't respond. Knowing him, he'd probably issued the warning and disappeared the next second.

When I turned back to the bed, Ellie's eyes were locked on me. "See something you like?" Putting my hands on my hips, I arched my brow and waited for her reply.

Ellie's face turned eight shades of red in five seconds. "Gavin, get dressed." She tossed my shirt at me from where it was lying on the bed.

"Lady, all this is yours, so look all you want." I crawled across the bed and kissed her lips while I pinched her nipple.

Her laughter was refreshing. I couldn't help but join in, and soon, we were both struggling to pull our clothing on quickly.

"Are you going to be all right down there? They are going to know what we did, and there might be some teasing." Pulling her to me, I looked into her eyes.

"As long as you stay close, I think I'll be fine." Standing on her toes she planted a quick kiss on my lips.

I unlocked the door but turned to her when I remembered something. "I didn't get to give you your gift." Reaching into the pocket of my jeans I pulled out the little box.

"I don't need a gift; you've given me so much—" Ellie's hands flew to cover her mouth when she looked down at my hand. "Gavin, that's too much. I can't accept that." She shook her head and took a few steps away from me.

"I don't do things halfway. You deserve anything I can give you." I reached for her hand and slipped the gold ring accented with a cushion-cut diamond onto her finger. It was three carats, and even the slightest hint of light made it sparkle and shimmer. I asked our jeweler for something that would brighten her day just as much as she brightened mine, and he sure did deliver.

The plain gold band I had given her before we left Montana nestled right in under the diamond, like it had been made for it. Was it over the top for a marriage of convenience? Yes. But I didn't care. For now, we had to make this believable.

Another quick knock on the door brought me back to the here and now. The door swung open, and my mother stood in the doorway, arms crossed and frowning.

"Listen, you may be newlyweds, but you will not ruin my Christmas supper. March." She pointed to the stairs. "If the two of you think you're going to be disappearing during the New Year's Eve gala like you did tonight, think again.

I will be watching you like a hawk." She pointed at Gavin and then pointed to her eyes. Her frown turned into a smile as she turned to walk down the hallway.

"Boundaries aren't big in your family, are they?" Ellie asked as she walked ahead of me out the door.

"Well. No." I shrugged as I followed her.

"Maybe you should change the lock on the door because it seems to me there are keys floating around." Ellie looked over her shoulder and sashayed down the hallway.

"You telling me there will be more reasons to lock the door?"

She turned and reached for my hand. "You can count on it."

Chapter Sixteen

GAVIN

New Year's Eve had become a special night for my family over the last few years. Mom had taken to hosting a gala to raise money for different projects in the community. My usually levelheaded mother buzzed around the house like a queen bee raking her hive.

Tonight was the big event, and everyone had their instructions, but the ball didn't start for a few more hours.

There was a knock on the door, and Tyler ran to get it. When he came back into the room, his face was ashen. Our uncle stepped through the door just behind him, wearing a scowl.

My father stood from his armchair. "Adam, what brings you here? Surely this is classified as slumming it for you." He walked over to Uncle Adam with his hand extended. Adam brushed past him linking his thumbs in his belt loops.

My mother's brother hadn't darkened the door of this ranch in at least a decade. A sinking feeling in my stomach told me I was probably the cause of his visit.

"Good to see you, Brian." He turned to my brothers and me and nodded. "And you too, boys. Color me impressed that you've all managed to marry off on the brink of forty. That's why I'm here. To see Gavin's marriage certificate. Tyler's marriage was odd, Rob never could stay away from Jessica. But you, Gavin, you're the wild card. You always have been."

The sinking feeling turned into a thud, but I wouldn't let him ruin the night for us. "Adam, I'm sorry, but we won't be entertaining this today. It's New Year's Eve, so whatever business you think you have here will have to wait." I walked up to the man, never breaking eye contact, and waited for his response.

"Gavin, are you telling me you're refusing to produce a marriage license so I can see the legitimacy of your nuptials?"

I cringed internally at the use of that word. Maybe it wasn't so much the word but the way it dripped like venom off his tongue.

My father stepped between us. "Adam, come say hello to Sandra. I'm sure she'd love to see you." He led Adam to the house but looked over his shoulder and gave the three of us a look that screamed fix this or else.

"What are you going to do?" Tyler asked when my father had gone inside.

"I don't know," I replied, rubbing my palm against the scruff on my face.

"Go get the marriage license. Simple as that." Rob looked between Tyler and me. "Guys, it doesn't matter how Gavin got to the altar, just that he did. Adam doesn't need to know that you only got married to keep Ellie safe."

My father appeared seemingly out of nowhere. His eyes were dark, and I could almost see the wheels turning in his head. "Your mother is making Adam feel welcome. Why? I'll never understand." He turned and headed out of the room again. When he got to the doorway, he turned and waved for us to follow, then continued without waiting for us to comply.

The second he was out of earshot, I turned to my brothers. "Look, no matter what happens, he doesn't find out about why I got married. Deal?"

They both nodded, and we followed Dad out of the main house and over to Rob's.

"Close the door, Gavin." Dad's words were short. It was winter. Did he really think I would just leave it hanging open?

"Gavin, I need to know. Is this marriage on the up and up?"

"Absolutely, Dad." Lying through my teeth didn't usually work out well for me. But it hadn't been going too badly over the past month. Ellie and I were getting closer. What had started out as a lie was feeling more like the truest connection I'd ever had with a woman. That had to hold some promise, didn't it?

"I've made a few calls. Why is it that nobody ever saw you and Ellie together? Not even late-night meetups at the cabin. If she's due in May or June, you would have had to be together in September." He walked over to the couch, sat, and waited for a reply, never taking his focus off me.

"You had someone watching the cabin? The entire time? You never trusted me, did you?" Walking over to him, I crossed my arms and waited. The deflection was a Hail Mary, but I had to try something to get the focus off my relationship.

"Of course I trusted you, but as much as I hate to admit it Adam's right about you being a wild card. You weren't completely reliable after you lost your business. I wanted to make sure it wasn't going to impact my business."

"So you didn't trust me to keep Montana afloat? Thanks for that vote of confidence." I headed into the kitchen. I didn't know how long I could keep this up, but I hoped to give myself a few minutes to regroup.

Tyler followed me. "Gavin, I don't think it was because he didn't trust you. He was just looking out for his assets after a few bad decisions were being made." Tyler chimed in and turned his back to dad. "Go with it." He mouthed to me.

"Well, I guess I should thank you all for telling me how you really feel. Making sure I know no one here trusts me. What am I doing now that gives you cause for concern?" That might not have been the best question.

"Nothing. I'm more than happy with the work you're doing here. You are more focused after marriage than these two jokers were." Dad stepped into the kitchen and pointed at Tyler and Rob.

"Thanks, I think." I shook my head while my brothers tried to hide their grins. "I'll run home and get the marriage license." I put my boots on and stepped to the door, but with my hand on the knob, I turned back. "Did you actually have me watched?"

"No. Well, for a month, yes. But you were doing so well. I knew I didn't need to continue keeping tabs on you." Dad looked at the floor and scuffed his foot over the hardwood. "Gavin, there's nothing I need to know?"

Shaking my head, I replied, "Nope."

"Okay, I'll deal with Adam." He nodded, and I walked out the door heading for home. "Find the certificate and come meet us in the den."

Somehow that had worked. I'd never been great at lying, especially to my dad, but he'd believed me—or at least decided to go along with the ruse.

I hadn't seen Ellie all day. She was busy getting ready for the gala. This wasn't her forte, but Jessica had insisted it was the best way to get money out of people was to make them feel special and do something out of the ordinary. A New Year's Eve Gala was always a wallet opener.

When I got to the house, I walked in quietly. I didn't want to disrupt Ellie's nap, and I had a few hours before I needed to get ready. As her pregnancy progressed, it was taking more and more out of her, and she'd taken to napping at least once, if not twice a day. I needed to deal with Adam and send him on his way so he didn't have any chance to ruin Ellie's night.

Ellie was sitting at her vanity when I tiptoed into our room. She yawned and stretched, like maybe she'd just woken up. Her red hair was cascading down her back, the ends loosely curled. Her green eyes studied me in the mirror, appearing more emerald with her makeup done.

"Is it that bad?" Her voice was quiet and filled with disappointment.

"What? No. Ellie, you're stunning." I moved behind her and placed my hands on her bare shoulders to get a good look at us in the mirror. She always looked stunning, but I'd only been gone for a few hours, and it was as though I'd come home to a completely different version of her.

I'd thought she looked like a goddess the very first day we met, but she was looking even more stunning. Nothing held a candle to my wife when it came to beauty. "I wish we didn't have to go to this thing." Bending low, I nibbled at her ear. "The only thing I want to do is take you to that bed and have my way with you." She tipped her head, allowing me access to her neck, and I blanketed it with kisses.

"Okay, that's enough." She laughed and swatted the hand I was snaking down her shoulder to the top of her breast.

"I'm serious, Ellie. I want to worship you tonight." I planted kisses on her neck and gently sucked on her earlobe.

She let out a sigh. "Would Jessica be mad if we didn't show up?"

"Furious. We'd never live it down."

"I guess we can't disappoint her then." Ellie turned on her stool and pressed her lips to mine. Breaking the kiss, she asked, "What are you doing home anyhow? I thought you were going to be busy all afternoon?"

"My Uncle Adam showed up." I needed more space between us if I was going to behave myself, so I backed up and sat on the bed.

"Oh, is this the guy you planned to fool when you tricked me into marrying you?" The grin that spread across her face was infectious, and I couldn't help but laugh.

"Yes, that one. He wants to see our marriage certificate. Do you have any idea where it is?" Relaxing back on the bed, I propped myself up on my elbows.

Ellie stood and walked to the dresser. She opened the top drawer and shuffled through papers, then pulled out the certificate. "Here," she said, holding it out as she stepped up close to the bed. "If he needs a copy, just ask your mom to do it. I don't want that out of our hands. I don't trust a man who's more than ready to pull the rug out from beneath his family."

"Thanks." I stood and kissed her again. Brushing my hand over her, I pulled the edge of the towel that she had wrapped around her, then I broke our kiss and backed up, watching the towel fall to the floor. "Oops." If I couldn't have a taste of her before we left for the gala, I needed a look to remind me what I was in store for when we got back home.

Scanning her body from head to toe, I lingered on her breasts. I wanted to assault them with my mouth while my hands roamed the rest of her body. But I'd have to wait. I took a deep breath. "Guess that will have to do until tonight."

Adam had found his way to the wet bar by the time I returned, and it sounded as though my mother had been making sure he knew how angry she was at him. In my entire life, I had only heard my mother raise her voice a handful of times, but she didn't seem shy about laying into her brother. The arguing stopped the second I stepped through the door, and all eyes turned to me.

"Here." I shoved the copy of our marriage certificate at him—I'd made sure to stop in my father's office to make the copy, because Ellie was right. I didn't trust him with the original. Crossing my arms, I waited.

He frowned and studied the document, then shoved it back at me. His eyes narrowed as he stepped into my space. "This is all a little—"

My mother cut him off. "Adam, you've worn out your welcome. How dare you come in here questioning the relationships of my boys. What happened to you? You were the best, most protective brother growing up, but you've become a money-hungry old man. Mamma would be so disappointed. You can leave." She walked to the door and opened it, giving him a pointed look.

Adam's mouth hung open and he walked out of the house.

"Now, all four of you men need to go get ready for the gala. If you aren't on time, you will be the next ones out that door," she said firmly before she stepped out of it herself and headed back toward the main house.

Chapter Seventeen

ELLIE

The big barn was lit up like a disco ball. Music wafted out from the open door, and people mingled out front.

I absentmindedly played with my bracelet while I watched the comings and goings of our guests. A coldness flowed through me and the pulse in my neck pounded as my heart raced.

The barn was filled with too many people I didn't know, and I couldn't force myself to walk in alone. It had been years since I felt like this.

Shy.

Overwhelmed.

I shuffled backward until I was far enough away from the open barn door not to raise suspicion, then I turned and rushed in the opposite direction.

Tonight's fundraiser was for the local hospital, and it was my introduction into the world of the Morton family. Their friends and important people in the community were milling about. I had never seen anything like this in my life.

Jessica had planned everything right down to the dress I was wearing. But it didn't matter how I was dressed. I was completely out of my league. I didn't belong there.

"Where are you going? Everyone is excited to meet you." Gavin walked up behind me and rested his hand gently on my lower back. His voice was low, and he smelled like cedar and honeysuckle.

He was dressed in a black suit jacket and wearing black wranglers. Over the few weeks we had been here, I had seen him in dirty jeans every day, which was a stark contrast to the man standing in front of me.

"Gavin, you look absolutely amazing," I breathed and took a step back to look him up and down. "Wow." Was all I could say.

"You done ogling me? Because I need to look at you." He stepped in close and ran his hand down my arm. His touch was light and sent tingles deep into my core.

"You are stunning. I can't believe you've been hiding yourself behind baggy pants and shirts."

"Well, I didn't want to flaunt the fact I was having a baby, and one that's not actually yours," I whispered.

Gavin leaned into me and matched my volume. "How many times do I have to tell you, I don't care about that?"

His warm breath tickled my neck and sent shivers down my back. I pouted my lips out a bit and looked into his eyes.

Gavin lowered his head and brushed his lips against mine, then he wrapped me up in his arms and pulled me close. Ever so gently, our tongues tangled, and he tightened his grip on me.

He pulled away and guided me to the barn. Gavin cleared his throat and shuffled his feet in the new dusting of snow. "Are you worried I might do something wrong? You seem a little jumpy."

Gavin gave me a half a smile before shaking his head. "Nothing you could ever do would upset me. You don't give yourself enough credit." He put a hand on my neck and stroked my cheek, then leaned in to kiss away my worries.

Footsteps sounded then, and someone cleared their throat. "Is the honeymoon ever over for you two?" Kate asked. Gavin and I parted and looked back to see Kate and Tyler walking toward us.

Gavin backed away from me. "Your lipstick is smudged," he whispered in my ear. I wiped around my lips. His low chuckle almost made me take him into the house to continue our exploration of each other.

"The crowd is looking for you. Would you like me to tell them you're preoccupied?" Tyler looked from me to Gavin. He knew the truth about our relationship, and he'd probably told Kate. They seemed to have the kind of marriage where there were no secrets.

"No, don't do that. We were just on our way in." I threaded my arm through Gavin's and nudged him toward the barn.

Kate leaned over to me and whispered, "That was not a 'we're pretending to be together' kiss. Are you two giving in to the chemistry between you?"

I was happy the sun was setting because I was sure I turned ten shades of red. "I don't know what's happening, but I hope so."

"We will continue this conversation tomorrow." Kate said as she walked back toward her husband.

The trip to the barn seemed quicker than I hoped. Kate and Tyler stopped at the door, and I took a deep breath as Gavin led me into the throng of people. We stood on the stage together. This was a Morton family event, and we were expected to portray a united front.

When we were all in place, Gavin's father spoke. "Ladies and gentlemen, we would like to welcome you to the New Year's Eve Gala. This year, our donations will be used to upgrade equipment at the hospital. As you all know, medical equipment is costly. We are honored to work with the hospital, and our ability to do so is because of your ongoing support."

The crowd clapped and Brian took a moment to let it die down. He was a born speaker. Brian commanded a room with very little effort.

"We would like to introduce you to the newest member of the Morton family. Please welcome Gavin's wife, Elyse Morton, to the family and to our community." Brian turned to me and held his hand out.

The crowd clapped, and I stepped toward Brian and plastered on the fake smile I'd mastered so long ago. But bile rose in my throat at Brian's use of the word community. It was nothing like the one I'd left, but it made me sick to my stomach anyway. I walked back to Gavin's side and squeezed his hand for dear life.

He turned and looked at me, and while his face didn't change much, his eyes held concern. I pasted on my best smile and turned my attention back to the crowd.

"Enough chatter. Now you know why you're here so, let's get dancing." Brian called as he handed the mic back to the band.

CHAPTER SEVENTEEN

The band started playing, and the crowd took to the floor. When I stepped off the stage, I was greeted by person after person. They introduced themselves, welcomed me to the community, and many already had donation checks ready for me.

"It's so nice to see Gavin has settled down, and with the most beautiful Morton wife of them all, if I do say so." A man walked up to me and handed me a check before he found someone to dance with.

The check had more zeros than I knew what to do with. Gavin appeared at my side and whispered, "How much did Haden pull from the vault?" I showed the check to him, and Gavin gave a quiet whistle. "He's always been very generous. Probably helps that you are gorgeous. He's a ladies' man."

I looked at Gavin and back at the check and smiled. "Is he? Maybe I should go see if he wants to dance." Arching my brow, I turned, pretending to look for the man that I now knew as Haden.

Gavin caught me by my arm and pulled me to him. "Not on your life, Elyse. I'm the one who gets to hold you tonight."

Instinctively, we swayed to the music. In Gavin's arms, I felt like everything in the world could only go my way. Everyone here tonight believed in me and, more importantly, Gavin believed in me. Nobody had had faith in me for a long time and it was nice.

The music stopped, and Sandra took the microphone. "Ladies and gentlemen, the funds are rolling in and as of right now we have raised just shy of seventy-five thousand dollars."

Kate snuck up to the front of the sage and handed Sandra a piece of paper.

Reading what she had been given, her face lit up. "Thanks to a generous donation that came in just before I took the stage, I can now update our total to one hundred and twenty-five thousand dollars. Thank you to New Dream Homes."

"You got it set up?" I whispered to Gavin.

The smile on his face said it all. The idea he had been mulling over in his mind since we'd arrived in Texas was finally being realized. "I went to the bank. They were confident I was a good investment based on my reputation and the fact that until my old business partner started making shady deals, I had plenty of capital. Once the legal stuff is over, I should retain my share of the funds, and they agreed."

Flinging my arms around Gavin's neck, I couldn't help but let out a little squeal. "I'm so happy for you."

"Let's dance," he whispered in my ear.

Chapter Eighteen

GAVIN

"Are you feeling up to a drive? We should go out and see what kind of shape grandpa's house is in." I leaned against the door, crossed my arms, and watched Ellie as she moved around the room. I couldn't tear my eyes off her.

"Sure, I think it would be good to get out of here." She set down the clothes she was putting away and gave the room a scan, her brow furrowed.

"Jacket?"

"Yeah."

"I have it. Come on, let's have some fun."

"You still know how to have fun?" She teased. Sure, I'd become a bit more serious while building my new business, and the demands of keeping my family happy on top of that were a bit much. But did it really seem like I didn't know how to have fun anymore?

"I'm fun." I pulled her coat from beneath mine on the hook and tossed it on the bed for her before closing in. "I'm too serious? Is that what you think?"

"Maybe..." She bumped into the wall behind her. There was nowhere for her to go.

"Maybe I just need help remembering how to have fun." She shut her eyes as I dipped forward, anticipating a kiss, but instead I gave her a firm slap on the behind. Ellie's eyes shot open. The action didn't seem to displease her, but she was shocked. "See, this old boy's got some surprises left in him yet. Let's go, Little Spoon."

The old house wasn't in terrible shape. It was a two-story white farmhouse with a wraparound porch. This house was a far cry from that of my parents and even my brothers, but there was something about it that felt like home.

I couldn't put my finger on it. Maybe it was the simplistic style or the memories it held, but I was happy to be there after so much time away. For years, I'd avoided returning. It was far easier to focus on life outside of the ranch than deal with the scrutiny of my family. I was more than happy to be on my own for decades. I looked over at Ellie. Somehow, she was changing all of that for me.

"What's wrong?"

"Nothing. It's just been a long time since I've been out here." I stared at the house in front of us. "Want to go in? See where you'll be living?" I tried to lighten the mood, but the grayness of the sky mimicked how I was feeling.

Ellie nodded and smiled at me. We hadn't overstayed our welcome at the big house, but it was time for some privacy, and the baby would need a nursery and she'd need a place to settle in to being a new mother.

With the cold seeping through my coat, I held my hand out for Ellie, and we ran to the porch.

A scent of chocolate chip cookies, apple pie, and Old Spice wafted through my nose when I pushed open the door. I knew it was just my imagination, but it felt real. My grandparents had been gone so long, it was impossible for those familiar smells to still be lingering, but it put me a little more at ease with this entire situation.

I watched as Ellie scanned the entry way. It was dusty, and the paint was peeling, but those were easy fixes. She wandered into the front room, a smile forming on her face.

"What's that look for?" I asked quietly as I came up behind her and wrapped her in my arms. She needed to be held, and I wanted to be the one to do it.

"There was a house that looked almost identical to this close to the ranch in Montana. The Hestmens used to own it. When things were bad at home, I could always run there, and Mrs. Hestmen would have cookies and a cup of tea ready for me." Drawing in a ragged breath, she continued. "Being in this room

CHAPTER EIGHTEEN

just brought that memory back. I'm sorry. I'm being a downer. Can we keep touring?"

"As you wish, ma'am. Let's check out the office. Then we'll go to the kitchen and proceed upstairs, where the magic happens." I waggled my eyebrows, expecting Ellie to turn red like she usually did when I said something like that. Instead, she exploded in laughter.

"I can't wait to see that. Lead the way Mr. Morton." She motioned ahead of her, and I walked out into the hallway, breathing a sigh of relief.

The stairs creaked as we moved to the second story, but those would be an easy fix. Three bedrooms and a bathroom occupied this floor. "Everything needs work," I mumbled as we wandered through the house.

"It just needs people, laughter, and love, Gavin. And we're here to do just that." She encircled my waist with her arms. We'd been playing these parts since we'd come to Texas, but I wasn't sure if this was that or if it was more.

I wrapped my arms around her, and we stared out the window of what would be our bedroom.

Standing there, we watched the sky go from a crisp dull gray to a hazy white. The wind picked up and rattled the windows.

"Oh no."

"What is it?"

"Blizzard. We're going to be stuck here until it's over. I better get some wood and get the fireplace going. It's going to get cold in here." Absentmindedly, I kissed the top of Ellie's head before I let her go.

"I'll see if there's anything to eat in the pantry." She was hot on my heels as I ran down the stairs. "If nothing else, I'll get the oven going to start warming this place up."

I stopped midstep, and she obviously wasn't paying attention because she plowed right into me, sending me flying down the last few stairs. #

I caught myself before I hit the floor and then caught Ellie as she stumbled into me.

"Gavin. I'm sorry." Her eyes were wide, and she flinched when I tightened my grip on her arm to steady her.

"Ellie, it's fine. It was an accident." I let go and took a step back, holding my hands out in front of me.

"Gavin, I am so very sorry." She took a few steps away from me like she was afraid I'd hurt her.

"Ellie, did he hit you?"

She shook her head. "No, but there were threats and manipulation. Flinching was just my way of protecting myself, waiting for it to happen."

I crossed the gap between us, and I took her into my embrace. "You never have to worry about that again. I'll never raise a hand to you or threaten to do so."

"I know you won't. You aren't that kind of man, but I can't always help the reaction." She spoke into my shirt.

"I know so little about your time in Montana. Will you tell me about it? The rumors, the flinching, the woman who was in my kitchen. What's the story? Maybe if I know more about your past, I'll be able to help you feel more comfortable with me." I reached out for her hand and guided her to the living room couch to have this conversation.

Once she was settled, I gave her a few moments. I wouldn't make her talk if she didn't want to. Crouching in front of the fireplace, I threw in the paper I had wadded up.

Her voice was distant when she spoke. "My father had a vision for a community where everyone worked together, shared resources and just wanted to live a life that provided well for families." Taking a ragged breath, she looked out the window across from her instead of looking at me.

"The people of the community looked to my father for guidance, and at some point, that went to his head. He heard about things that were happening in large cities and didn't want outsiders infiltrating our group, so he made sure the women of the community were sheltered at home. Teams had been arranged to go to town for supplies when needed, but unless you were part of that group, you didn't leave."

She lowered her head, wringing her hands in her lap before she continued, and I couldn't stand the idea of not touching her, comforting her, as she spoke, so I sat beside her on the couch.

"When I was younger, we could leave the compound, but then, almost overnight, it was forbidden. The penalty for leaving was shunning for a week. Each offense after that would be a week added on. When I got my fourth violation, no one spoke to me for a month. Except Ray. He had been so nice, and

I'd been so thankful for the company, but then turned on me at the end of my month. I had to confess in front of the entire community that I had disobeyed our leader by speaking to Ray. They accused me of luring him in. That's when they decided I would marry Ray. That way, according to them, he would keep me under control."

My blood boiled at the images her story created. The hatred I was beginning to have for the life Ellie had been living was growing rapidly.

"Marrying girls off who were 'trouble' was my father's answer. So that's how I ended up engaged to Ray. My father never raised his hand to anyone, and his punishments were harsh, but they were consistent. Ray, on the other hand, would fly off the handle if I looked at him wrong, if I laughed at him or dared cross him about anything." She stopped talking and wrapped her arms around herself.

When she didn't continue, I placed a gentle hand on her knee. "I want to fly to Montana right now and deal with your father and Ray myself." Clenching my fists, I took a few deep breaths to calm myself. How could anyone treat another human like that? Especially one like Ellie. She was a beautiful woman who deserved the world.

Chapter Nineteen

ELLIE

We sat in silence until Gavin's stomach rumbled so loud I was sure his mother heard it. "Why don't I get us something to eat?"

"I'll ever say no to that. Would you like some help?"

"No, I'm fine." I stood and went to see what snacks I could find. The kitchen was surprisingly well stocked for being vacant.

"Gavin, who lived here last?" I called as turned on the oven.

"I think one of the hired hands stayed here a few months ago. He was married with a family, so mom put them up here so they could have their own space." He stopped at the entryway and answered my question before braving the storm to get more wood.

We had pulled the couch as close to the fireplace as possible and sat together, not saying a word, as the room warmed and ate the crackers I had found in the pantry.

Gavin rested his arm on the back of the couch behind me, and shifting slightly, I leaned into him. He moved his arm to wrap around my shoulders and pull me to him. "I will never let you feel like you did in Montana. You're safe here Ellie., I have wanted to tell you that from the moment we set foot here."

"What took you so long, then?"

"I was afraid you were too vulnerable and might break."

"Just because I looked like a helpless girl in Montana, doesn't mean I am one. I've had to learn to be tough."

"I'm learning that." He pressed his lips to mine. The sparks that had been present since the night he kissed me in front of my father erupted, heating me from the inside.

I repositioned myself so I straddled his legs, and Gavin rested his hands on my thighs. The warmth radiated to my core as he slid them until they were resting on my inner leg.

"Did I see a fireplace in the bedroom at the top of the stairs?" I whispered between kisses, relishing the feel of his arousal beneath me.

"You are very observant, and is that a hint? Should we move locations?"

"It might be more comfortable." I let my head fall back as Gavin attacked my throat with trailing kisses.

"Let's go. I will grab the wood."

"Oh, I plan on grabbing some of my own very soon," I said as I shot him a look over my shoulder on my way out of the room.

I giggled at his reaction. Gavin's mouth was open, and I thought his brain might explode.

Running up the stairs this time, I needed to get the room ready. The big bed had a drop cloth covering it, just like everything else in this house. When I pulled off the cloth, I found the most beautiful double wedding ring quilt I had ever seen. My mother was a quilter, but as I looked at this piece of art, I was in awe. This was done by someone with great care and attention to every detail.

"I thought you would be naked by now." Gavin's low voice turned my attention away from the quilt.

"Well, I didn't want to be presumptuous," I teased, reaching for the buttons on my shirt.

Gavin tried to load the wood into the fireplace without taking his eyes off me, but it wasn't working. He fumbled and dropped a log on the floor in front of the hearth.

Walking over to where he crouched, I undid the last button, pulled my arms out of the sleeves, and let the shirt fall to the floor beside him.

He struck a match and lit the paper he had tossed into the fireplace, and the heat instantly warmed the chill that was creeping in. Or maybe it was the heat of his gaze warming my body.

With both hands behind my back, I unhooked my bra and slid the basic white bra off my body. Never in my life had I wished for sexier lingerie, but now I wished I'd worn something that would have blown his mind.

Standing, Gavin reached out and took my breast in his hand. His palm engulfed me, and the feeling sent tingles to my core.

In that moment, a new me was being formed. I had opened up about my life; we had crossed a different threshold in our relationship. I wasn't a woman who would put up with being told what to do anymore, and I was going to enjoy myself in the bedroom—or wherever I damn well felt like it. Now was the time to experiment with life and love.

Gavin moved his hands to the waistband of my pants. He popped open the button and slid down the zipper. "Ellie, I would love to take this slow and explore every inch of you like we did Christmas Day, but I'm afraid that once you're out of these jeans, I won't be able to control myself." He dipped his hand into my pants and slowly moved his fingers, pressing on my clit and making me moan.

"We can take things slow the next time. Please, Gavin, take me now." I hoped me begging him wasn't a turnoff. My ex hadn't liked it when I told him what I wanted.

Sliding my pants down my hips, Gavin watched me, the fire in his eyes burning hotter and hotter. When I was naked, he picked me up and laid me down on the bed. The sound of the snaps of his shirt popping open heightened my senses further. His shirt was quickly discarded, and he moved to his belt. Pulling the buckle out of its secure hole, he gave it a yank and then dropped it to the floor.

Ever so slowly, he unbuttoned his pants and lowered them, along with his underwear, to the floor.

The mattress shifted as he lay beside me. "Was that a good gasp or a regretful gasp?" He whispered as he made circles around my nipple with his finger.

"That was a oh god, you look even bigger than before gasp."

"Don't worry. You're going to be more than ready for it before I even try." Slowly Gavin moved his hand down to my center, then slid one finger between my folds while finding my delicate bud with his thumb. He made gentle circles over it while sucking a nipple into his mouth. I arched my back, wanting more.

This wasn't for his benefit; it was for mine. Gavin's touch was deliberate, and he knew what he was doing.

A moan escaped my lips as he slipped a second finger inside me. "I guess you like that." He said before he pressed his mouth to mine.

My entire body was on fire. It had built slowly at first, a spark of heat growing hotter. Gavin pushed his palm over my mound and stroked until every part of me was ignited.

"Gavin please. Please." I wanted him in me. I wanted more than his fingers. We needed to be one. He spread my legs wide and sat up. Before moving on top of me, he took my nipple in his mouth again and gently nipped it as he sucked. I ran my hand through this hair and sighed.

"I think you're ready." His voice was low and thick with desire. Positioning himself at my entrance, he ever so slowly ran his shaft up and down my pussy.

In one motion, he plunged into me, and I cried out in ecstasy.

"Are you okay?" His voice was concerned, and his eyes bore into mine.

"I've never been more okay." Pulling him to me, I kissed him with wild abandon. Tongues swirling and fighting for space.

Gavin pulled back and buried himself to the hilt again and again. I forgot what day it was, that there was a blizzard and where I was. Sizzling passion flowed between us as I teetered on the brink of total pleasure. I didn't want it to be over, but my body had a mind of its own.

A blinding climax ripped through me, and I cried out. Gripping the sheets in my fists, I moaned again as another wave washed over me. Gavin moved faster and his breathing increased. Sweat formed on his brow as he stiffened and groaned and emptied himself into me.

Collapsing on top of me, he nuzzled my neck. "That was amazing," he whispered in my ear before he rolled off me. Resting his arm on my stomach, he took my breast in his hand and let it rest there.

"It felt like I was being made love to for the first time." I smiled sleepily at him, then realized what I'd just said. Closing my eyes, I willed my pulse to slow. Did I just say make love? That was a little presumptuous. Had I ruined the moment? "Gavin, I didn't mean make love. I should have just said had sex."

Chapter Twenty

GAVIN

I listened to Ellie's quiet breathing for a while, then slipped out of bed and added another log to the fire. The room had warmed up nicely. The fire in the front room should probably be stoked, but I didn't want to leave her.

I sat on the hearth and stared at my wife. Our marriage had solved the problem of getting her out of Montana, and I'd needed a wife to save the ranch from falling into the hands of my uncle. What I hadn't counted on was the way my feelings for her were growing.

This life was not the one I had dreamed of, but it was the one I had, and there was no one I would rather spend it with than Ellie. She stirred, so I stood and walked back to the bed.

I lay beside her again, and she wrapped her arms around me and put her leg across mine. We hadn't been intimate since Christmas and she still tried to keep to her side of the bed most nights, but she always woke up in my arms. I'd been dying to worship her again for so long, but I knew she needed more time to adjust to this new life we were living. After today, though, maybe we could live like real husband and wife rather than two people who had come together due to circumstances. The wind continued to howl outside, and the windows rattled occasionally, but we were warm and out of the weather. This could be a comfortable home for us for the time being.

An hour later, Ellie woke up and shifted in my arms. "Are you getting up?" I murmured.

"I should make dinner." She turned and sat on the edge of the bed. Her smooth back made me want to reach out and touch her.

"Maybe you should just come back to bed." I ran my hand down her spine.

She sat up straighter and looked over her shoulder. "You think I should? What are you going to do to me this time, husband?" She arched her brow and smiled slyly at me.

"There is so much I want to do to you." Moving my hand to her hair, I ran my fingers through it. "You are the most beautiful woman I have ever seen. I was incredibly lucky to find you standing at my stove."

Her laughter rang through the room. "Then you'll be even happier to find me standing at the one in our home. As much as I would enjoy coming back to bed, I'm starving." Falling back on the bed, she kissed me, then stood and sauntered out of the room. Naked.

"Aren't you going to put any clothes on?" I called out after her.

"What's the point? They're just going to come off again." Her voice grew quieter as she descended the stairs.

I stared at the ceiling and grinned at her antics, but my father's words rang through my ears as I lay there. I was risking a lot by starting this new business and risking my part of the ranch. I was going to have to work ten times harder and be on top of every transaction going through this company.

Taking a ragged breath, I flipped the blankets off and pulled on my underwear and shirt, then headed for the main floor. In the short time she had been downstairs, Ellie had gotten something simmering on the stove, and it smelled incredible.

Leaning against the doorframe to the kitchen, I watched her move with ease and grace. She had found an apron and slipped it on. I couldn't help but stare at her wearing nothing but that damn apron.

"Something smells good." I stood over her shoulder as she stirred whatever she had cooking. "Looks good too." I ran my hand across the round fullness of her ass.

"Don't make me find a wooden spoon, Gavin Morton." The smile that crossed her face as she looked at me made my heart jump.

"You're going to have to fight me for use of that spoon, missy. Your backside exposed to me would make the perfect target." Before I backed away, I gave her a light swat.

Ellie yelped and tried to push me away, but I was already out of arm's reach. She lifted the pot off the burner and set it on the opposite side of the stove top, then turned.

I slowly backed out of the kitchen, and she stalked toward me. "You know, Mrs. Morton, you could wear the apron and nothing else every day. I wouldn't complain."

"Well, you can be sure I'll be fully clothed then. You're insatiable. I would never get any work done." She giggled and put her hands on her hips.

This stance made her baby bump prominent in the apron. Somehow, I hadn't really given it much thought until now, but I couldn't resist resting my hand on her abdomen. It was fascinating thinking about how her body would change.

Ellie walked into my arms and turned so I could place both hands on her stomach. She sighed as she relaxed back into me.

"Is it heavy?"

"No. I expect it will be eventually, though." With her head on my shoulder, she closed her eyes and breathed quietly.

"What are you thinking?" I murmured.

"For one moment just now, I forgot what my life really is, and it really felt like we were a family." Her voice trailed off, and she tensed up in my arms.

"We are a family. Maybe not in the normal sense, but I'm here for you." Tightening my arms around her, I wondered who I was turning into.

Chapter Twenty-One

ELLIE

"Gavin, I'm heading out," I hollered up the stairs. There was no reply. I looked at my watch again. Kate, Jessica, and Delaney were seconds from picking me up. I didn't need any grand gestures from Gavin, but a little acknowledgement that I was leaving might be nice.

The crushing sound of the gravel on the road alerted me to my approaching sisters-in-law.

"Okay, that's it. I'm gone."

"Wait. I heard you the first time," Gavin said, jogging down the stairs.

"And it was too much effort for you to say anything?" Shaking my head, I grabbed my purse off the bottom step.

"Have a good time. Maybe we'll catch up with you ladies along the way." His smile was annoying. He could charm the pants off anyone, but right now I was ticked off at him.

"We'll see." I walked out the door and hopped in Kate's SUV.

"Let's get girls' night started," Jessica said as we pulled away from the house.

"Please. I need this more than you realize." Sighing, I relaxed back into the seat and watched the Morton family "compound" whiz past.

Had I only traded one "community" for another? I wasn't shuttered away here and could come and go as I pleased, but it felt like someone was always watching my every move.

The only time I felt truly free was when I was alone in the house.

"Things not going well, Ellie?" Kate asked, looking at me over her shoulder from the passenger seat. Her brow was furrowed, and a genuine look of concern was clear on her face.

I had to come up with something. "Oh, you know, newlywed kinks to iron out. I don't know if either of you realize, but Gavin is a stubborn man."

All four women laughed as if I had made a hilarious joke. "Ellie, the Morton men are the definition of stubborn, and they learned it at a young age."

I could see that streak in each of them, but somehow, I was sure Gavin had been given an extra dose.

"Enough about the guys. Are we ready to have some fun?" Delaney asked as she pushed the gas pedal harder, and we sped down the highway.

"Yes," Jessica and I replied in unison.

The neon sign for the bowling alley glowed brightly in the evening light. I'd never been much for bowling, but in a small town you take what you can get. And what I was getting was a night out with the girls away from Gavin. We had been getting to know each other since we had moved into our own home and that meant many interludes during the day. I wasn't complaining. Gavin was a great lover, but a night with the girls would be a reprieve.

"All right, ladies, let's get this party started," Kate cheered as she turned the vehicle off.

"Clearly we need to get out more." Jessica replied dryly.

The place was packed, but one lane remained open because Kate had reserved it. With shoes in hand, we strutted over to our lane and started our evening.

I was happy to see none of us were going to be the next champion bowler. Every gutter ball resulted in hysterics and high fives. We were the life of the alley.

"We'd heard Gavin had gone and gotten married. But I never imagined a girl as pleasant as you would put up with the likes of him." An older woman with blueish hair laughed and patted my arm from the opposite end of the bench we were seated on.

I wasn't sure if I should be flattered or offended. But it was giving me a little insight into the man that had suddenly become my husband.

"Looks like Ellie won this game, and let me tell you, it is still a pathetic score." Jessica pointed at the big screen above our lane.

"I'm sure it has something to do with the fact I'm the sober one." Shrugging, I giggled. "Hand over the keys, Kate." I extended my arm and held open my hand.

She willingly handed over the keys, and we returned our shoes and headed for the truck.

"Time to hit the bar. We've got a DD and babysitters, so let's take advantage of it," Jessica said as she hopped into the back seat.

"Drive," Kate demanded, so I did just that.

I hadn't been to the bar since arriving here. To be honest, I hadn't been to a bar at home either. It was against the rules of the community. I could hear my father's commanding voice saying nothing good ever happened after eight. The community shut down at seven thirty. People stayed home. Very rarely did families get together in the evening.

The place was packed tonight. A nervous energy filled me as I listened to the music blaring from inside the building.

"Tyler texted. The guys will be here in about an hour." She linked her arm through mine, and we headed in.

Jessica scoped out a table where a group of people were putting coats on and heading for the doors, so we made a beeline for it.

Once we were settled, Jessica took drink orders from us and was off to the bar.

Couples swayed on the dance floor, each in their own bubble, like the world around them didn't exist. I had never seen anything more mesmerizing.

"Here are the drinks." Jessica returned carrying the beverages. She set them down without spilling a drop and lifted her glass. "To our first girls' night out." We raised our drinks in unison and clinked glasses.

"Care to dance?" Turning to look at where the voice came from, I stared into the face of a brown-eyed cowboy with a sweet shy smile and dimples that would charm the pants off any woman.

"I'm sorry I don't dance," I replied.

"I'll teach you." There were those dimples again. "All you have to do is put one foot behind the other." He took my hand and guided me toward the dance floor.

How bad could it be? He seemed nice enough, and the girls hadn't objected, so he was probably an all right guy.

"All you have to do is remember quick, quick, slow, slow. See? Easy. And don't think too hard about it. That'll will mess you up. Ready?"

I nodded, but I was nowhere near ready. The next song started, and of course, it was something quick. This cowboy, whose name I hadn't caught, twirled me around the dance floor like a pro. I was obviously not the first girl he had taught to dance.

When the song ended, I was winded, and he walked me back to my table. "Thanks for the dance. I might just find you for another. You did great." He tipped his brown hat and walked off toward the bar, his Wranglers hugging his ass in an exceptional way.

"You looked like you were having a blast." Kate said as she leaned over to me.

"It was fun." I shrugged and took in our surroundings. "Where's Jess?"

"She went to line dance over on the other side of the dance floor." She pointed. and

I caught a glimpse of Jessica's blond hair as she twirled. "Why don't you go dance?"

"I'm only interested in dancing with one cowboy, and he'll be here shortly." She beamed. I wondered what it would be like to love someone as much as she loved Tyler.

The man I'd danced with earlier reappeared at our table a couple of songs later. "Hey, Kate, mind if I take your friend off your hands for a few minutes?"

"Not at all, Lee, go right ahead."

He held his hand out to me. Before I knew what I was doing, I took it, and he led me out to the dance floor.

Again, the music started, and we whirled around and around.

Suddenly the man let me go and I was staring into the eyes of my husband.

Chapter Twenty-Two

GAVIN

Ellie and I danced until the song finished, my arms wrapped tightly around her. I didn't want to cause any more of a scene by walking off in the middle of a song, but I was livid. When the music paused between songs, I guided her through the crowd and outside the bar.

"Just what do you think you're doing?" I asked when we were a safe distance from the door.

"Dancing. Having a good time." She shrugged and grinned.

My blood boiled at her cheerful response. "You're my wife." I emphasized wife and pointed at my chest. "You don't go around dancing and flirting with other guys. I saw you dance with Lee. You couldn't keep your eyes off each other." I was clenching my jaw.

"Lee, was that his name? He was really nice."

"Elyse, you're mine."

"Really Gavin? Have I given you any inkling that I wanted someone else? If I remember correctly, since we moved to the farmhouse we've been horizontal every day." She leaned in and whispered, "sometimes more than once a day. So save the macho attitude. Your cock is the only one I want."

I took a few steps back from her and put my hand over my mouth. Shaking my head, I let my hand fall. "Ellie, I'm sorry. I didn't mean to." My voice trailed off.

"Whatever this is," she waved a hand between us, "isn't normal." Ellie's voice dropped to almost a whisper again, and she closed the gap between her body and mine. "I'm not asking that we pretend we're in love like Tyler and Kate, but can we at least try to fool the town and your family?" Ellie raised her arms and let them fall back to her sides.

"I would like that." Smiling softly, I held my hand out for Ellie to take. "Care to dance?"

It took her a minute, but when she returned my smile, my heart all but leaped out of my chest. We walked back to the table where the rest of the group was waiting.

"Now that your lovers' quarrel is over, we have a round waiting." Rob threw his arm around me. "Don't try to pretend there wasn't a problem. We all know you have a piss poor poker face."

I shrugged his arm off and grabbed a glass from the table. "I have to take my woman for a spin around the dance floor."

Never letting go of Ellie's hand, I led her to an empty space on the floor. She was too far away from me for the slow song playing, so I pulled her close and wrapped my arm around her tighter.

"You're tense. Just relax and sway to the music," I whispered in her ear.

The tension left her body as she melted into me. We moved together and I couldn't help the elation coursing through me.

I buried my nose in her hair, the mix of lavender and strawberries filling my senses. Until this moment, I hadn't noticed what shampoo she used or that the scent of her perfume had permeated all my dreams.

I had missed the fact she was working her way into my soul. It wasn't calculated on her part; she was just going about her life as she normally would while also making mine incredibly easy.

Was this what normal couples felt like? I had always imagined marriage as hard work, but being with her was no work at all. Having her standing beside me made me want to give this a try.

"You know, I never imagined I would have a wife, and this is obviously not the most ideal situation, but I want to try. You have provided the friendship I didn't know I needed, and I want to give our marriage a real shot." My words were quiet. I didn't need the entire bar knowing our conversation.

Ellie rested her head on my shoulder, and we stayed that way until the song was over. Was that confirmation? Or was she working out a way to let me down? I would have liked some type of acknowledgement since I had just poured out my feelings.

She looked up again and pulled my head toward hers. Our lips met, and the passion ignited between us. For one brief moment, I forgot we were in public, and our tongues battled for control. Whoops and hollers went up from our table and broke the moment. Ellie ducked her head and smiled shyly. The blush that crept up her face made me want to take her to the truck and have my way with her this instant.

"Sorry," she whispered, playing with a button on my shirt nervously. "I just felt like the moment called for it."

"I'm not sorry at all, and I wouldn't be mad at more of those moments." Arching my brow, I took her hand and pulled her off the dance floor.

Lee, the cowboy from earlier, stopped beside our table. "I guess I lost you before I even got you," he said to her before he looked at me. "Morton, this one is special. You hurt her and I'll be there to pick up the pieces."

I held out a hand to him. "I won't hurt her, but there's nobody else I would rather know has her back than you."

As the night continued on, the drinks flowed, and we took turns teaching Ellie to dance.

When the bartender announced last call, we all looked at our watches.

"Wow, where did that evening go?" Tyler slurred.

"Who drove tonight?" Ellie looked between the four of us.

Nate raised his hand.

"Hand over the keys." Palm out, she made a grabby motion.

Nate was a good friend of ours. We'd known him almost all our lives, and he worked directly for our family on the ranch. He'd recently married Delaney, Kate's younger sister.

With Nate's keys in hand, Ellie pointed to the door. "Morton family, you all need to get home and into bed. March." Her voice was commanding and sexy. Was it the beer, or was I finding my wife irresistible tonight?

Turning on my heel, I followed her orders to the letter. I marched out the door grinning at the idea of my wife being so bossy. My brothers and their wives fell into step behind me, and I turned in time to see Ellie shake her head at the lot of us.

The ruckus quieted a bit after we dropped Nate and Delaney off. Rob and Jessica were next, then we pulled up in front of Tyler and Kates. "Get out. Get out. I'm going to puke." Kate climbed over Tyler and ran for the bushes in her front yard.

"And on that note, I think I'm going to walk home." Ellie climbed out of the SUV and handed Kate's wallet to Tyler. "Can you walk, or are you sleeping here tonight?" she teased.

I stumbled out of the truck and grabbed her hand. "I'm sober enough to walk my wife home. Good night, Ty." I waved as I headed off with Ellie.

"Look at the stars," I said as the lights from Tyler's yard faded behind us.

"It sure is beautiful. Nothing hidden by hills or mountains. It's freeing, less sinister here." Ellie slipped her hand out of mine and put space between us.

"What do you mean, sinister?" I asked as I caught up with her.

"The mountains hide things its occupants don't want the world to know about." Her voice was soft, full of pain.

I put a hand around her wrist, halting her movements. "Want to talk about it?"

"Not really. I just never knew how free I'd feel being away from there." She ducked her head.

"I'm sorry life was hard and I'm sorry I have been making it harder lately." I rested my hand on her lower back and leaned down, brushing a gentle kiss to her lips in the moonlight.

As if my hands had a mind of their own, I lowered them to her ass and pulled her as close to me as I could with clothes on.

Chapter Twenty-Three

ELLIE

The weather changed, and the sky turned dark. There was a dampness in the air that, if I had been in Montana, I would have interpreted as a sure sign that a blizzard was on the way. The door swung open, and Gavin walked into the house. It was unlike him to be home now.

"Hi, what's going on?"

"I have to help Rob and Nate bring in a bunch of cows. They need to be brought in before this blizzard hits. The weatherman said it might be a few days." He walked over to the coffeepot and poured himself a cup, then topped off the one I had out on the counter. "I need to get some warmer clothes on, and I wanted to let you know I was heading out."

"Thank you for thinking of me. I hope you won't have to be out there long." I took a sip of my coffee, watching him do the same.

"You should have enough wood to last if the power goes out and I'm not back. Keep the fires going in the living room and bedroom. Kate will come get you if I am not back tomorrow. There's no reason to stay here alone."

"Tomorrow? Will it really take that long?"

"It shouldn't, but if we get stuck out there at the cabin, I have no way to let you know. If the power goes out, use the radio to keep up with the weather updates." He looked around the kitchen. "I don't know if there's anything else to tell you. This isn't your first blizzard, I guess."

I nodded. This all seemed like a lot of what ifs and maybes. I bit the corner of my mouth and turned to look out the window. He was right. This wasn't the first blizzard I had been through, but it was the first where someone else was relying on me to keep going. Letting my hands rest on my stomach, I took a deep breath.

Gavin moved quietly behind me and wrapped his arms around my shoulders. "Don't worry. I'll be back before you have time to miss me."

"Promise?" I whispered, leaning back into him.

"I promise. I have to go, but I'll see you soon." His words were quiet, and I could tell he wasn't looking forward to the job ahead of him. After kissing the side of my head, he left me standing alone.

His quick footsteps above me filled me with uncertainty. I didn't need to be coddled, but this was a side of Gavin I hadn't seen before. He was tense, his face held more emotion than he even realized.

Stomping back down the stairs, he looked like he was wearing five layers of clothes under his coveralls. "Here, take this." I handed him his coffee in a go cup.

"Thank you. See you soon." He lifted his hand to my neck and ran his rough thumb across my cheek, gently pulling me toward him and covering my mouth with his hungrily.

It felt like I was kissing him for the last time. Is this what it felt like when frontier women sent their husbands off on long roundups? Was I being dramatic? Quite possibly. But I held on to him tighter until I heard boots on the porch.

"Gavin, come on. We need to ride. Let your wife go. We will be home before she has time to miss you." Nate had popped his head in the door. "Hi, Ellie."

Breaking our kiss, I looked over Gavin's shoulder. "Hi, Nate. Keep my man safe."

"Will do, ma'am." Smiling, he nodded and backed away from the door.

"Be safe, cowboy."

"I will." Stealing one last quick kiss, he turned and walked out the door.

I watched him swing his leg over his horse as I walked out onto the porch. The three men waved as they rode off. When I couldn't see them anymore, I turned back into the house and closed the door to the building cold.

The hours passed, and the wind picked up as the snow fell. I sat in the living, watching the storm gradually obscure the trees that surrounded the house until they were no longer visible.

My landmarks gone, I'd never felt more lost than I did at this moment. I placed a few more logs the fire, the sparks exploding like fireworks in the fireplace. Immediately, I felt the warmth of the new logs now ablaze, and as I turned, the lamp beside the couch flickered and went off.

"Well, isn't that just great?" Placing my hands on my hips, I looked around, mentally making a check list of everything I needed to do.

Check the fire in the bedroom was first on the list.

The minutes ticked by like hours. The house had remained warm, thanks to the almost constant back and forth checking. Rummaging through the hall closet, I found a set of pie irons. It might to be a five-star meal, but I was going to have as much fun as I could riding out this blizzard alone.

Opening the fridge, I pulled out the ham and cheese, then searched for pizza sauce in the pantry. I had the makings of a campfire pizza.

My watch read eight o'clock as the storm raged on outside the window, and I desperately looked for an outline of the three riders.

I stood at the window until my legs were tired, then slumped onto the couch and pulled the big quilt up to my chin. I watched the flames flicker and listened to the hisses and pops of the burning logs as I drifted off.

A cold blast of air filled the house. I startled awake and looked toward the fire, but between the hearth and me stood a large man with his back to me. Then someone was screaming.

"Hey, it's me. Quit screaming. Ellie, it's just me." He came toward me with arms extended, but before I could pull away, the flames from the fireplace lit up his face. Gavin.

I slapped my hands over my mouth to stop the scream I'd been ready to let loose. He pressed his lips together, his eyes lighting up, and I couldn't help but start to laugh.

"You don't have a wooden spoon under that blanket, do you?" Gavin was obviously seeing similarities to the night we met, and I couldn't help but lift the blanket and reach under like I might just pull one out and threaten him with it.

"No, I don't" I giggled.

CHAPTER TWENTY-THREE

"Good, as cold as I am, you just might shatter me into a million pieces."

Hopping off the couch, I flung my arms around him and held on for dear life. "You should get out of these wet clothes."

Chapter Twenty-Four

GAVIN

The winter turned to spring, and the ranch was buzzing with new life, green grass, and blooming flowers. Ellie and I grew closer every day. We had become friends quickly and now we were more than that. She and I worked well together, and I enjoyed her company when it was just the two of us.

Stepping out of the hardware store, I set off toward the pharmacy, realizing I should have asked Ellie if she needed anything while I was here. I had my phone halfway out of my pocket when someone called my name.

"Gavin."

I turned, coming face to face with a ghost from my past. She was someone I used to think I'd never get over, but seeing her now, I realized I hadn't thought of her once in the last few months.

"Naomi, hi."

She flung her arms around me and hugged me tight. When she finally let me go, she was almost vibrating with excitement. "Are you busy? Let's grab a coffee somewhere."

I looked around the street, which was usually bustling with people, but it was almost empty. "I suppose I could spare a few minutes."

"Good. Let's go to Stella's. I want to hear all about what's been happening. I heard you got married! That must be a story." She laced her arm through mine and pulled me toward the coffee shop.

CHAPTER TWENTY-FOUR

Had she always chattered this much? Naomi had always seemed so levelheaded, but this encounter had exhausted me already.

"Hey, Stella. Two coffees, please. We'll be in the back booth." Naomi said as we walked past the older lady at the counter.

"I'll grab them. You go get settled,"

She walked to the farthest booth while I waited for Stella to pour the coffee.

"Here you go. And may I just say how lovely your wife is? She came in the other day, and we had the loveliest conversation. Much better choice than that one." She tilted her head at Naomi. "You dodged a bullet there." She arched her brow and gave me a knowing look.

"Thank you, Stella. Ellie's still settling in here, and I know she had a wonderful visit with you. Thanks for taking the time to make her feel welcome." Taking the coffee off the counter, I couldn't help but feel like everything Stella had said was the truth.

"Don't do anything to hurt that wonderful woman." She put her hands on her hips and stared into my soul.

"I won't. I promise. This was an ambush. I will be in and out before you know it." I gave her half a smile, hoping she knew this was the last place I wanted to be.

"I know, dear. I saw everything." She turned back to the coffeepot and began changing the filter and grounds.

I stopped and set the cups down on the table before I sat down across from Naomi.

"I guess I don't have to ask what you've been doing since we broke up." Naomi picked up the mug and raised it to her lips.

"Yeah, well, life keeps moving." Hopefully keeping m answers short would end this conversation quickly.

"Mine didn't I was heartbroken for months. I picked up the phone almost every hour to call you." She set down her cup and reached out and put her hand on top of mine.

Pulling my hand away from hers, I put it in my lap. I didn't need anyone gossiping about the two of us more than they already would. Things were changing between Elie and me, and our marriage was becoming more real every day.

I was feeling far from obligated when it came to Ellie. I could see us growing old together, raising our kids and building a life here.

"Gavin, what are you thinking? You're not dad material. We always said we never wanted kids. Traveling, not being tied to one place, that's what you always dreamed about."

"Again Naomi, things change."

She wasn't wrong. I'd never wanted kids and here I was about to raise one that wasn't even mine.

"She trapped you, didn't she? Saw your money and got knocked up on purpose."

There was so much Naomi didn't know but had Ellie trapped me. Had she sought me out because of her situation? Was this always the plan? Her father seemed to give up rather easily. Were they all in on it?

Naomi kept chattering on, but I tuned her out. My thoughts were all over the place. I needed to get home and get to the bottom of it all.

What were the requirements for an annulment? Screw an annulment. I didn't care if I had a divorce to my name. This wasn't exactly a normal situation.

"I have to go. Thanks for the chat." Before I left the table, I stopped and looked at her. "Naomi, we are done. Whatever you hoped to accomplish here only solidified the fact that I am over you. Don't bother me again." I watched her face fall and tears well in her eyes. I didn't give her the opportunity to plead her case. I just walked away and didn't look back.

Once in the truck, I grabbed my phone to call Ellie but decided against it. This conversation needed to happen face to face. How afraid for her life was she really?

I had always been too trusting when scared women were involved, but I hadn't over offered to marry one of them.

Chapter Twenty-Five

ELLIE

"Why did you come to my cabin that night? You knew who I was, and you wanted to use that to your advantage, didn't you?" Gavin slammed the door behind him as he stormed into the house.

"What are you talking about?" I looked up from the pile of laundry I was folding and stared at him.

"Was your family in on this also? It's no secret my family is wealthy. It would be the perfect ruse."

He stood before me, fists clenched at his sides, his hair in disarray, like he'd been running his fingers through it.

"Wha—"

But he cut me off before I could ask what on earth he was going on about. "You got knocked up by some guy you had second thoughts about and needed to run away. And somehow you knew about me and that cabin. Did your friend Matt tell you about my family? Was he in on it? Anyone else, and you would have been stuck going back to Ray. But I'm the fool who fell for your sob story." He paced the kitchen, flinging his arms wildly.

I had never seen him like this. Even after a fight with his father or disagreement with his brothers.

"I didn't plan any of this. I wouldn't have gone back to Ray, no matter what. If you hadn't found me, I would have been on my way to figuring out life on my own." I looked at the floor in front of Gavin's feet. How could he think so little of me? And where was all of this coming from?

Our morning had been wonderful, and the months that we had been in this house had been amazing. We'd fallen into our routines. Working with Kate and the horses we were rescuing and watching Gavin figure out his own dreams was more fulfilling than anything I'd ever done in my life.

"I'm staying at the main house tonight."

As fast as he had walked into the house, he was gone again. Should I go after him? Or should I give him some space? What on earth led him to have these thoughts?

Turning back to the laundry, I sat down and cried. What was he going to do? Would he throw me out?

Honestly, I wasn't all that surprised that he didn't want to see this through. I knew this ruse would have a time limit, and here we were. Gavin and I had been having fun playing house, but I was far too young for him and pregnant with another man's child. Of course he'd finally come to his senses and realized he didn't want me.

Glancing up at the clock, I knew I needed to get to town to grab a few groceries and the mail that I had forgotten to ask Gavin to pick up. The post office closed in an hour, and I had a package waiting, so I dried my tears and went to the kitchen sink to splash some cold water on my face. I was glad it was a thirty-minute drive to town, because I was sure my eyes were puffy and my face was splotchy.

"Oh Ellie, just the person I wanted to see today." The woman behind the counter smiled as she turned to the mailboxes. "This just arrived for you." She handed me a letter.

"Thank you, Mary. I will remember the key one of these days. My brain seems to be a million other places." I laughed and smiled at the older lady who had run the post office since the Morton family moved here. She took great pride in telling me how long she had been the postmistress.

"You look about ready to pop, so it's no wonder you're forgetting things. I remember a few days before I had my last. I couldn't keep a thing in my head." Her soft voice made me feel a little more at ease.

"Thank you so much for this, Mary. I hope this little one arrives soon." Turning to leave, I flipped the letter over and opened it, then I headed for the truck.

Pulling the mysterious letter out of the envelope, I unfolded it, and my blood ran cold the instant I recognized the handwriting.

Elyse,

You think it was that easy to get rid of me?

I know where you are. You look so beautiful pregnant with my child. There is no way that man will be raising any offspring of mine.

Don't worry. I'll be there to bring you home soon. Gavin Morton better watch his back because I don't take kindly to him running off with you and my baby.

I will involve your father and brothers to bring you home if I have to. They've been watching, too.

Ray

The letter shook in my hand.

I remembered vaguely what happened last time someone from the community ran off and was found. She lived a horribly lonely life. Nobody would look at her, much less befriend her because she had brought shame to her family. I didn't know how I got to the truck, but I was sitting in it when my phone rang.

It made me jump, and I fumbled around as I dug through my purse to find it. Gavin's name flashed on the screen. But what if it wasn't Gavin? What if Ray had gotten to him already?

I had done this. I had involved Gavin, and now he and this baby were in grave danger. My only option was to run, but where? I doubted Gavin would care much, but I didn't want his blood on my hands.

I would be running for life if I took off. No, I had to go to the police. There was no other option. To run would be a black mark on Gavin and the Morton family, and I couldn't just abandon the family that had taken me in when I didn't have one of my own.

Gavin would worry if I didn't answer, so I hit the green button to answer.

"Hello?" Trying my best to keep my voice chipper and carefree.

"What are you up to?" He sounded remorseful, and I wondered if he would actually apologize for the way he acted earlier.

"Just in town. I had a few things to grab, and I will be home soon." A knife felt like it had been driven through my heart. I was lying to the man I was in love with. But it was a lie to keep him safe, so I had to be forgiven for that, right?

"Okay, well, I was concerned when I saw you drive out of the yard, so I thought I would check in."

"See you soon. Gavin." My voice was quiet, and I hoped he wouldn't sense that anything was wrong.

"Bye," he replied, and the line went dead.

Tossing my phone in my bag, I backed out of the parking spot and went toward the police station.

Running was not the answer, and I wasn't sure the police would do much. That left one option. To go back to the ranch and let the Morton powers that be handle the situation. Gavin had saved me once, and maybe with the full force of his family behind him, he would be willing to do it again.

I pulled a quick U-turn at the end of the street and headed back to the ranch.

A black pickup suddenly appeared behind me, the sight ratcheting up my heart rate. As it pulled closer to my bumper, I waited for some kind of impact, but the truck sped around me and disappeared on the horizon.

Saying a silent thank you to whoever or whatever was watching over me, I let out a long breath, hoping it would slow my pulse.

But before I had made it to the ranch road, a blue truck sped up behind me, riding my ass. I let off the gas so he could pass, but the truck matched my speed, so I accelerated back up to the speed limit, but it stayed the same distance away.

Looking in my rearview mirror, I saw the man wave. I knew that wave. My blood ran cold, and I started shaking again. It was Ray.

How was I going to get out of this? I couldn't stop. I didn't trust him to remain calm. What would he do when I was supposed to turn into the ranch? I didn't want to lead him there. My stomach sank when I realized I didn't actually have a plan.

Ray sped up and pulled in front of me. He slowed until I had no choice but to stop. He had blocked the entire road. The ditches on both sides were almost sheer drops to the creek.

Ray stepped out of his truck, and the smug grin on his face made my stomach turn. A vehicle pulled up behind me and for a moment I thought I was saved, but Ray nodded to the driver. When I turned, I saw my oldest brother. Ray wasn't working alone.

I let my head fall to the steering wheel, and I closed my eyes.

"Open the door, baby. We have a lot to talk about." Gone was the haughty look on his face. His eyes turned black, and he clenched his jaw, giving me a murderous look.

"I don't have anything to say to you."

Bringing his hand up, he slammed the side of his fist on the window. I let out a scream, but he only laughed.

"The faster you open this door, the better this will go for you. Unlock the door, baby."

"I'm not your baby."

"Oh, you were mine first. Don't forget that. The child you're trying to pass off as a Morton is mine. I'm the one who put it deep inside you."

"Get out of the truck. We're going home."

"I am home Ray. My home is with Gavin, not you." I wished my words had sounded as strong out loud as they had inside my head.

He pulled a tire iron out from behind his back and smashed out the back window. "I told you this could go the easy way or the hard way, and you've just chosen hard." He reached in unlocked the door.

"Hi honey, nice to see you." He snarled as he opened the door.

This was it, time to face my hangman.

Chapter Twenty-Six

GAVIN

I watched Ellie drive out of our yard and leave the ranch as I walked to the barn. She wouldn't have had time to pack her things, so she must be coming back. Seeing her eyes full of hurt made me immediately regret the tone I had taken.

Why had I let Naomi get to me? Finding Rob alone in was rare these days. His job managing the ranch was getting busier than ever before, but I needed to talk to someone.

"Hey can we talk?"

He looked up from the stall he was fixing. "Sure. I'm due for a break." He motioned for me to follow him over to the stack of hay bales. "What's up?"

"Addison. How did you...?" My voice trailed off. I had debated this conversation in my mind for days.

"Move past the fact that she's not biologically mine?" Rob asked, looking down at the straw and pulling out a piece.

"Yeah. How did you know?" I looked at him and waited for a reply.

"You're predictable Gavin. And I figured eventually we would have this talk." He arched his brow.

There was nothing I could say to that. Rob knew me better than I knew myself at times.

"So what's bothering you, other than the obvious?"

CHAPTER TWENTY-SIX

"I ran into Naomi," I said.

"Ahh, well, now things are making sense. What did she say that got to you?" Rob glanced at his phone when it chimed, turning the sound off and setting it face down beside him.

"She reminded me that we broke up because I didn't want to settle down and I didn't want a family. Now here I am doing the things I never wanted, and for a stranger, no less."

"She's not exactly a stranger anymore, Gavin. Jessica and I see the way you look at each other. It may not have started that way, but you've both grown." He leaned back against the bale behind him and looked off to the other end of the barn. "You love her. I can see it in you. Tell her, be her husband and be the dad to that baby. I had eight years with Addison was mine before I found out she wasn't mine. But there would have been no way to stop loving her, even if I'd found out sooner. You get to be the man in that baby's life. Love that baby and his mom, and there will never be a question again about you being a father."

"Thanks, need help here?" I asked.

"Good thing you asked, because I was just going to start barking orders."

The ringing of my phone made me aware of the time. Ellie should have been home an hour ago. I watched her leave while I was looking for Rob. When I talked to her, she said she needed a few things, but that shouldn't have taken long. Even with traveling to town and home, she should have been here by now.

"Hey, Danny, what's up?"

"I wish this was a personal call, but we found Ellie's out on the old highway just south of the police station." Danny was silent for a moment before he took a deep breath. "Gavin, the rear driver side window had been broken out. We found a tire iron at the scene. The driver's door was open, and Ellie's purse and phone were inside."

"Where is she?"

"We don't know that yet. The surveillance cameras outside the precinct are being reviewed, but so far, we've got nothing. Can you tell us how long ago she left?"

"About two hours ago. I called her, and she said she had a couple things to do before she left town. She always gets the mail last."

"All right, I will send someone to the post office and see if we can narrow down a time. We have officers out looking, so hang tight until you hear from me."

"You're asking me to sit on my hands while my wife and baby are missing? You've lost your mind."

"There's protocol to follow, Gavin. At least give us an hour."

"Thirty minutes and I have a chopper in the air." I hung up the phone before he could respond.

I ran to my truck and sped over to my parents. Rob hopped in with me, and Tyler was already there working on some pasture management. Dad was always close by. Bursting through the door, I almost ran into Mom. "Where's Dad?"

"He's in Tyler's office. Gavin, what's wrong?" Her face had changed from happy to see me to concerned in a split second.

"Come with me. I will tell you all at once." I took off toward Tyler's office with my mom on my heels.

"Ellie's gone," I shouted when I burst through the doors.

The three men looked at me with blank looks on their faces. My mother covered her mouth with her hands.

"What do you mean?" my father asked.

I collapsed onto the couch and hung my head into my hands. "Danny called. One of the officers found Ellie's truck parked on the highway. Someone busted out a window with a tire iron."

This was all so strange. We had left Montana months ago, and we hadn't heard a word from anyone there. So who around here would want to hurt Ellie?

"Do the police have any leads?" Rob asked.

"No, nothing. I gave Danny thirty minutes, then I'm heading out with the chopper to look. I better call the airstrip." I heaved myself to standing, but Tyler pushed me back onto the couch.

"I'll do it. Sit."

"We haven't had any threats recently. There would have been some chatter if there had been any attempts," Dad said as he sat down beside me.

The minutes ticked by, and I was getting more anxious by the second. I stopped my leg from bouncing and checked my phone at least once a minute, hoping to hear from Ellie.

"I'm not waiting any longer. Let's go." Dad stood and headed for the door. My brothers and I followed.

"Bring our girl and grandbaby home," My mother called after us.

Mom was right. Ellie belonged here, and I had been an idiot to doubt it.

Chapter Twenty-Seven

ELLIE

Just over the Oklahoma border, Ray pulled over. I thought maybe it was the perfect time to jump out. Running wasn't my forte right now, but I was sure I could outsmart him.

As I went to grab for the handle, a shadow came across the window. I looked up into the face of my brother John. He pulled the door open. "Get over."

I slid over, and my stomach lurched at my proximity to Ray. There was no escaping now. Looking over at John, I hoped to see something of brotherly love or even compassion, but there was nothing but a blank expression.

Ray sped off, and I felt like I was shrinking into nothing the further from Texas we were getting. Think, Elyse. How do you get out of this? Nothing was coming to mind. It was as if I had lost all ability to think rationally.

John leaned on to the side of the door and closed his eyes. That was their plan. To drive the entire way without stopping. Maybe I could pretend I was in labor. I wasn't due for a few more weeks, but I could convincingly pretend, and once they took me to the hospital, I could get away.

That was it.

"We aren't stopping, except for fuel. If you go into labor, you're delivering this kid in the truck," Ray snarled. It was as if he could see inside my head. Was I really that predictable?

CHAPTER TWENTY-SEVEN

The hours passed, and I was never alone. I could see the headlines in the local paper.

Ellie Morton Ran Away from Her Life.

All sympathy would be given to Gavin when people found out his "wife" had run off with another man. A man whose baby she had been carrying. I was sure every woman in town would fawn over Gavin, and there would be no shortage of interested parties to fill my place. What place had that been? Friends with benefits? Legally, we were husband and wife, but that could easily be done away with by an annulment. Gavin could make a case that I had tricked him into marriage.

"So what have you been doing on your lengthy vacation? Playing the dutiful housewife?" Ray's laugh was evil.

Closing my eyes, I shook my head.

"No, housewife isn't up your alley, is it. Whore? Have you been whoring around with that man? Your body sure loves pregnancy. I can't wait to get my hands on you again." Ray took his eyes off the road and gazed at my breasts.

"Ray, cut it out. While I don't condone her decisions, she's my sister." Wow. John was still willing to acknowledge me as family.

"What do you care?" Ray spit out.

"I said knock it off." John raised his head and looked over me at Ray. This could be the undoing. Maybe John wasn't as determined as Ray was to get me home.

The silent drive was nerve-racking, I had been grippingly my hands so tightly, my fingers had started to go numb, and I was sure the inside of me cheek would be raw for days from chewing on it.

Just before we left Oklahoma, Ray and John switched spots. I was tired. I wanted to close my eyes, but I was afraid to. What would Ray do if I let my guard down? My ex-fiancé rested his head on the doorframe, his breathing changing, and he started snoring.

Breathing a sigh of relief, I looked out the window and watched as we crossed into Colorado. Making a mental note of the time, I tried to keep things straight in my head, blinking fast to keep myself from nodding off.

"Sleep, Elyse. You need to. I will make sure he behaves." John's words were quiet, like he was trying not to wake Ray up.

"Why are you doing this?" I whispered.

"Sleep, Ellie." He was done talking, apparently.

I rested my head on the window behind me. But I longed to be sitting beside Gavin on our couch. He always knew when I was tired and made sure his shoulder was available to rest on.

Sleep came easy, but kicks from my little football player woke me up. I groaned, and John shot a concerned look at me.

"Just a kick. I've been sitting too long, and this little one isn't really happy. He likes to be moving."

"He?" John's brows raised, and I could have sworn there was a smile, but with only the moon and the glowing dash to illuminate the cab of the truck, I couldn't be sure.

"I don't actually know, but I have a feeling it's a boy." I looked down at my stomach and sent up a prayer for the safety of this baby. I prayed that no matter what happened to me, Gavin would find him and raise him.

We made it Montana in just over a day, and all I heard was grumbling because I made them stop more than Ray wanted. What could I do about it? I was a very pregnant woman stuck in a vehicle for hours at a time.

"Hank, were back," Ray called from outside my parents' home.

The house hadn't changed much, although it looked more dilapidated than I remembered. I slid across the bench seat and set both feet on the ground.

"This is what you had to go do?" my father asked when he saw me. His expression turned angry as he turned to Ray.

"I got her back. We can be married, and I can be back in good standing." Ray was almost pleading with my father.

"You think we have concerns about you because Elyse left and married another man?" My father was shouting now. He walked off the porch toward Ray. "You've lost standing because somehow you managed to pull the wool over our eyes. There are four children running around this community who share your DNA and you're doing nothing to help any of them. Apparently now five, given the size of my daughter. Elyse, get in the house."

I walked past John, who held his head in shame, and walked by my father, who never even gave me a second glance. Would my mother be happy to see me, or would I get the same silent treatment from her also?

CHAPTER TWENTY-SEVEN

"Hi mamma," I said as I walked through the door.

She turned, and a smile crossed her face. "Oh, my girl, I was worried I would never see you again." Tears filled her eyes as she walked over to me. It was then she noticed my expanded waistline. "Hmm, Gavin's?" she asked. Her voice was hopeful and fearful at the same time.

All I could do was shake my head.

"Well, he'll raise it as his, but you have to get out of here." She scanned the room, her gaze landing on the key hook beside the door. Rushing to it, she rifled through the multitude of keys until she found the one she wanted. "Here, take my car. It has a full tank of gas and it's right by the road."

The keys felt cold in my hand as I looked at them. "Mamma, I love you."

"Shh, child. I know. As sad as I was to find out you were gone from me, I was relieved that you had escaped. Life here wasn't meant for you. I didn't know how to get you out then, but I know how to now."

We froze when we heard footsteps on the porch stairs. "Put the keys in your pocket," she whispered.

I did as I was told, and we waited.

Chapter Twenty-Eight

GAVIN

The hours ticked by. There was no sign of Ellie anywhere. Night had fallen hours before, but I couldn't rest. Couldn't turn off the worry and the regret. I wandered to the barnyard and looked up at the sky. I argued with the man upstairs, pleaded with Him, made deals hoping it would be enough for her to call me.

I promised to be the best father in the world, to love Ellie until my last breath and beyond. We would go to church every Sunday. But the phone never rang.

I watched the sun peek over the horizon from the porch steps.

My father came walking out of the house. "Have you slept?" He asked.

I shook my head and stood.

"Son, you need to rest."

"I can't. She's my life, Dad." My voice cracked. "This isn't a life without her and our baby. It's my fault she left in the first place."

My legs no longer capable of sustaining my weight, I fell to my knees. I ran my hand over my face, wiping away stray tears I hadn't realized were rolling down my face. "I had coffee with Naomi, and she filled my head with all the doubts I had about our former relationship. So I came home and started questioning Ellie about why she was here and why she was with me. She doesn't know how much I love her, and she doesn't have any idea how much I need her," I yelled as my father knelt down and pulled me to him, letting me cry into his shoulder.

CHAPTER TWENTY-EIGHT

My family gathered around me, and Tyler and Rob helped me to my feet. Mom rushed ahead of us when they dragged me through the front door and poured me a cup of coffee.

"Drink this, my baby. You're going to need it." Her voice was calm and soothing, like it had been when I was a child.

The warm liquid was a bitter reminder of the day before and the reason I'd treated Ellie badly. I was about to confess to everyone what happened when my phone rang. Picking it up, I hit the green answer button.

"Ellie?" I frantically asked.

"Is this Gavin Morton?" the voice on the other end asked flatly.

"Who's asking?" I barked.

"Hank Bowers, Elyse is here in Montana."

"She's what?" I yelled into the phone.

"Ray found her in Texas and brought her home. Quite frankly Morton, she ain't our problem anymore. She's your wife, so you need to come get her before anything happens." His voice was emotionless, like he was talking about dirt instead of his daughter.

"There better not be one hair out of place when I see her, or I will personally see to it that anyone involved in her abduction is dealt with. That includes you, Bowers." I was seething, my words spoken through gritted teeth. These last twenty-four hours had been torture.

"Gavin, everything ok?" Rob called from the other room.

I shook my head and looked at my family. "Ellie's in Montana."

I didn't need to say more. My brothers were hot on my heels.

Over the years, we'd had our ups and downs. But when push came to shove, they were the only men I needed standing behind me.

They were both on their phones, looking for information on the way to the truck.

"We have Tony on the way, and Tyler filed a flight plan. By the time we get to the hangar, it will be ready. The three of us will go with you. Mom and Kate can keep the ranch running, and Jessica will make sure the kids are occupied." Rob was beside me, matching my steps.

"I can't lose her or the baby."

"Gavin, we'll get her back, and the baby will be fine."

"I want the chance to truly make her my wife, I want to be a daddy to that baby." Words I hadn't spoken aloud for anyone else fell from my lips.

"What are you talking about? She's your wife, and that baby is yours." Dad looked over his shoulder at me and then to Tyler.

Tyler shook his head. "You better fill him in while we drive, Gavin."

Hopping into the truck, I knew it was time to come clean. So I told my dad about the night I found Ellie standing at the stove in my cabin. About her father and Ray and how we'd lied about being married.

"What was the endgame? What about when she was ready to move on and have a real life? Her taking off would have killed us all. You really don't think, do you? And all this is a result of a story you concocted?"

I nodded, feeling like I was three years old, being scolded. "You know, Dad, I never wanted to be a father because I didn't want to turn out like you. So you can be mad all you want. But over the last six months, I have realized that no matter what, I will never be like you." This was not the time to make grand statements or have this conversation, but my mouth was moving, and I couldn't stop it.

"I know I'll never live up to Tyler or Rob in your eyes, but I carved out a life for myself with little help from you. I've made mistakes, but Ellie is all the good that has come out of it. I will raise that baby as a Morton, whether you choose to be a part of our lives or not. This is my family we are talking about, and I need to bring them home."

"Well, let's go get our family, then." He turned off the ranch road and sped down the highway.

Flying over Texas as the sun set was usually one of the things I loved most, but I couldn't enjoy it tonight because people I loved were in danger.

My phone rang, and I answered it through my headset.

"Hello?"

"Gavin Morton?"

"Yes, that's me."

"I'm Lieutenant Sampson. I'm calling about Elyse Morton. Are you her husband?"

"Yes, sir," I said, my chest constricting at the seriousness of the officer's voice.

"She's been in a car accident. She is being life flighted to Billings."

"How is she?"

CHAPTER TWENTY-EIGHT

"I'm sorry, sir. That's all I know. If you have more questions, I can give you a number to call."

"Yes, that would be great." I grabbed a pen and wrote the number on the back of my hand. I ended the call and tapped the button for the flight attendant.

"Divert to Billings. Ellie is being taken to the hospital there. She was in an accident." I turned to look out the window to hide the flow of tears running down my cheeks. I had caused all of this by questioning her motives.

Waiting was the worst part. We were only an hour into our fight. Two more hours would feel like days.

The hospital staff was less than helpful. They kept telling me they couldn't give me more information until the test results were back. Even my questions about the baby went unanswered.

"Gavin, what's going on?" My father walked into the waiting room.

"They still won't tell me anything."

"You know, there was something funny about you and Ellie right from the start. Your mother felt like we were watching a relationship grow, not one that had been going on for months. I told her she was imagining things. That it was because you'd been gone so long. Man, I hate having to tell her she was right. I never hear the end of it. She's going to be okay," he said, sitting beside me and patting my knee. "What are you going to do next? She's going to recover, and you're going to have to make a decision about where to go from here."

"I'm going to marry her again. We'll have a big wedding and raise that baby as ours. Dad, I love her more than my own life." I rested my head in my hands and let the tears flow again.

My father moved his hand to my back and soothed me like he had when I was a little boy. Back when life was easy.

"I see the way you look at her and I am pretty sure she feels the same, so if this is what you want, we'll make it happen." He took a deep breath and slowly let it out. "So when she pulls through this, and she is back on her feet, it looks like we'll be hosting another wedding. Your mother will be happy. She was a little upset you eloped."

"What if she's not all right?" I looked up at him, no longer hiding my tears. Fear was creeping in, and every terrible scenario filled my head.

"She's going to be fine. I know it. The women my sons have chosen to spend their lives with are strong and resilient. The future of our family is in good hands with them." He looked from me to Tyler and Rob. "You boys have made me and your mother incredibly proud."

My brothers looked at each other and then looked at me.

I sat up straighter and looked at our father. "You hit your head or something, Dad?"

My brothers tried to hold back their laughter, and I couldn't help the grin that formed across my face.

He just shook his head and swatted my leg, and the three of us burst into laughter.

The waiting room door swung open, and a police officer walked through them.

"Mr. Morton?" he asked.

I stood, and then my father and brothers did as well. They formed ranks around me, and we waited for whatever he was going to say.

He held out his hand, and I shook it. "Mr. Morton, I am Sergeant Tillerson. Your wife was involved in a traffic accident. Would you mind if we had a seat?"

Once we were all seated, the officer took a deep breath. "She was being chased by a man named Ray Watson."

"Her ex-fiancé."

The officer nodded. "Yes. She was able to tell us the story while we were waiting for the paramedics to stabilize her and he baby. Mr. Morton, Ray's dead."

Chapter Twenty-Nine

ELLIE

The beeping beside me was enough to drive me crazy. I tried to roll over and turn off whatever was making the noise, but a pounding in my head and a sharp pain in my abdomen stopped me. My hand flew to my stomach, where a flat expanse greeted me.

Tears welled in my eyes when I realized what it meant. All these months I had been looking forward to bringing this little person into the world and it had all taken from me by his or her father. My pulse raced, the beeping echoing around the room sped up, and the nurse came running in.

"Mrs. Morton, you need to calm down." Her voice was reassuring, but I needed to know what happened to the baby.

"Where's my baby?" I whispered through gut wrenching sobs.

"Relax and open your eyes, Elyse." Her voice was soothing, and I relaxed a little.

Slowly, I opened my eyes and looked at the woman with black hair that was graying at her temples. She had kind brown eyes lined with crow's feet.

She was smiling at me and surely if something terrible had happened, she wouldn't be smiling. Right? With a nod, she directed my attention to the opposite side of the bed, where Gavin was sleeping, reclined in a chair with a baby on his chest.

My tears fell for another reason now. They were both safe. They were both here with me. Gavin's soft snores reminded me of that first night we had spent together when he became my knight in shining armor.

The nurse walked over to him and tapped on his shoulder. When his eyes fluttered open, she pointed at me. "She's awake."

Holding on to the baby, he sat up in the recliner and studied me. Gavin usually kept his emotions very close to the vest, but his eyes glistened with unshed tears as he looked at me. "Hi."

"Hi. Do you hate me?" I asked, looking away from him, afraid to know the answer.

"I could never hate you. We can talk about it later, but right now we have a baby to name." Standing, he brought the mystery bundle to me and placed the swaddled baby on my chest. "I'd like you to meet our son," Gavin whispered before he kissed me.

"A boy. I was so worried I lost him." I looked down at his perfect nose and lips. "Maybe you should take him back. He seemed to be happy with you."

"We've been supplementing with formula, but the nurse says he's going to need to learn to nurse soon. And frankly, it's impossible for me to do that." His eyes sparkled as he teased me. "What should we call him? I didn't feel right about naming him while you were sleeping."

"You could have. I wouldn't have second guessed you." The smell of this brand-new baby filled my nose, and I nuzzled his head. "What were you thinking of calling him?"

"Benjamin Paul Morton."

"I love it. Are you sure you want him to have your last name? It makes you tied to him and me for a very long time." I looked up at Gavin, searching his expression.

"I was going to wait until you were home to deal with a lot of stuff, but you should know. Ray died in the accident."

"He did?"

"Do you feel up to telling me what happened?"

Nodding, I took a deep breath and groaned.

"Take it easy. You've got a couple broken ribs," Gavin said, giving me a half smile.

CHAPTER TWENTY-NINE

"When I got to my parent's dad didn't want me around and my mom just wanted me to get back to safety. She gave me the keys to her car, and I snuck out the back door while everyone was eating supper." I licked my dry lips.

Gavin noticed and poured water from the pitcher on the bedside table and handed it to me. My mouth felt like someone had stuffed it full of cotton balls. But the cool water soothed it almost immediately.

"I don't know how far I got, but out of nowhere, Ray's truck was behind me. I had that car going as fast as it could go, but I couldn't shake him. After that, things are fuzzy. I know he rammed the back of the car, but after that, everything went black," I said. The images felt more like movie scenes than what I'd just lived through.

"You were almost to Billings. That's where we are now. The accident investigator said that when Ray hit you the last time, his truck hit the embankment at the ditch and about rolled six times. He wasn't wearing a seat belt and was ejected from the truck."

Sitting there looking at the baby on my chest, I couldn't muster up any sympathy for Ray. That man knowingly put me and the life of this baby at risk, and he didn't care.

Gavin leaned forward in his chair and whispered, "so, the other thing is, I want you to be my wife. I wanna have a big wedding and a party. I want you to get the *to have and to hold* forever, the big white dress, a honeymoon, and all that stuff."

Tears sprang to my eyes at what he was telling me. Gavin and I had settled into a great routine together, and somewhere along the way, he'd become the love of my life. I'd hoped he felt the same way, but on that last day in Texas, I was sure he no longer wanted me or the child growing inside me. What he was saying now, knowing Ben and I were what he wanted, elated me.

"Are you sure? I have caused a lot of trouble." I had to know if he was doing this out of obligation.

"Elyse, Ben has my last name, and I want you to have it too. I mean, you already do, but I want you to be my wife for real. Not just on paper. I have never been more sure of anything." Taking my hand, he squeezed it and looked like a kid on Christmas morning.

"Yes!" A smile formed on my face when his eyes lit up.

He leaned over and kissed me as the nurse walked in.

"Well, you two love birds, there is a waiting room of people who want to see this sweetheart. Would you like me to send them away?" She leaned against the doorframe and smiled at the us.

"They can come in," I said.

She left the room, and within seconds, the chatter of the Morton men echoed down the hallway.

The three men walked in, and their hard shells visibly melted.

"I get him first." Brian stepped close and patted me on the shoulder. "I am glad you are okay, dear. Welcome to the family officially. Now give me my grandson."

I handed Ben over to his grandpa, wondering how much Gavin had told him.

I looked over at my husband.

"While we were waiting for you to get out of the operating room, I told him everything." He shrugged.

"And he came clean to us the day you both showed up at Morton Ranch," Rob added in.

These men would fight to the ends of the earth for their family, but they had to one up each other any time they could.

"You're not upset with me for getting him in to this?" I scanned the four men, but none of them seemed to be concerned.

"Ellie, you brought Gavin back to us. His mother and I are grateful to you, no matter the circumstances around you coming into our family." Brian, who had made me nervous when we first arrived on the ranch, just might be the calm father figure I had needed my entire life.

Things between Gavin and his dad hadn't always been good, which was part of the reason he had been gone so long. But the man holding my son loved his grandkids without measure, was thriving with all of his sons at home, and had three daughters-in-law who didn't mind giving him a run for his money if he needed it.

"Jessica wants to know when the wedding is so she can get to work." Rob said as he tucked his phone back into the pocket of his shirt.

"How about August?" Gavin said, his eyebrows raised and a radiant smile on his face.

Chapter Thirty

Ellie

"Are you ready to escape?" I looked up from my book to find Gavin standing at the door with the most beautiful bouquet of white roses. "Those are stunning."

"I should have left them in the truck, but I wanted you to see them right away," he said as he strode toward my hospital bed and planted a kiss on my lips.

A noise came from the door, and we broke our kiss.

"Ready to leave?" The nurse asked, smiling.

"Yes, very ready. No offense."

"None taken." Her laugh was light. She went over all the paperwork and helped me move from the bed to a wheelchair.

Once I was settled, Gavin laid Ben in my arms. "They'll just let us leave with him?" I whispered.

"What else are we supposed to do? Stay here forever?" He chuckled and rolled me out of the room and down the hall toward the exit.

"Maybe until he walks?" I pressed my lips together to keep from laughing as we went through the doors to the truck Gavin had rented for the drive home. "He's so little." I looked down at him once more before Gavin took him from me and buckled him into the car seat. "Wow, you look like you've been practicing."

"Kate gave me a lesson a few weeks ago when the car seat arrived. Poor TJ wasn't impressed with me." Reaching for my hand, Gavin helped me up, and I walked to the truck and gingerly climbed in.

"Ready?" Gavin asked as he jumped into the truck and turned it on.

I nodded, but I wasn't ready for anything. How was I supposed to be a mother? Navigating everything with Gavin was going to take a lot of work. What if this didn't work? Could I be a single mother?

"Hey, stop. You're going to be a great mom. You've got a community of people rooting for you and willing to help," he said.

I grimaced at the use of the word community.

"Sorry." Gavin cringed. "A village? Is that better?"

"Not really." I shuddered and shook my head.

"How about a family? You aren't going to have a moment's peace. Mom already wants to move in and help until you're back on your feet. Dad is already shopping for a pony for Ben." Gavin looked ahead and pulled out of the hospital entrance. Navigating the city streets with precision, he took my hand as we pulled out on to the highway. "And you're stuck with me too. I know we have a lot to talk about, but the one thing I can say is that you'll never have to doubt my love for you or Ben again."

Gingerly reaching over, I put my hand on his leg. "I never did question it, Gavin. I was confused, yes. But I knew you would have to deal with a lot of emotions. And honestly, I have to admit, I thought the freak-out would have come earlier. From the moment you saved me in Montana, I never questioned your feelings."

He grabbed my hand and steered us toward the hotel.

"Tyler and Rob flew home this morning, and Dad is checking out now. I couldn't talk him out of driving home with us." Gavin looked at me and smiled.

"I don't blame him. He probably won't get any time with Ben once we get home and your mom, Kate, Jessica, and Addison get their hands on him." I couldn't help but feel at ease with the amount of love my son had from people who had no blood relation to him.

The drive back to Texas took three days. Gavin was determined not to make me sit in the truck for hours at a time. At one point, as we crossed into Oklahoma, I was begging to just keep going. I wanted to be home, and I longed for my own bed.

As we drove under the ranch sign, I breathed a sigh of relief. "I'm home," I whispered, not thinking anyone would hear me.

"Yes, you are, my dear. There's nowhere else in the world you belong more than here." Brian reached over the back of the seat and patted my shoulder.

"Thank you," I said.

Through tear-filled eyes, I watched the main house come into view. There were blue balloons adorning almost every part of the front of the house. A large Welcome Home sign was strung from pillar to pillar across the entrance.

The entire family was waving wildly as we parked. Tyler opened my door and helped me out of the truck. "You look worse than you did in the hospital." He said as he helped me up the stairs.

"Well, thanks a lot, I missed you too." I gave him a big smile. I didn't dare laugh for fear of doubling over in pain.

"Brian Morton, you get out of that truck and hand over my newest grandson." Sandra hollered as she knocked on the window.

Brian opened the door and handed Ben to his grandmother. Kate and Jessica rushed to her side to get a glimpse of the newest Morton. "He's absolutely perfect." they cooed.

"Enough standing out here. Let's get in the house. Ellie looks like she's about ready to fall over." Brian said. "Come on dear. Let's get you settled somewhere comfortable. You can even have my spot on the couch. It's the best place to nap."

I sighed and leaned on Brian as I moved toward the house. The first time I had entered this home, I was scared, alone and worried I wouldn't be accepted. Today, as I crossed the threshold, I knew I was loved like a daughter, and accepted as part of the family.

"The town was in constant vigil when word got out that you were gone," Sandra said as she sat down beside me. She never once took her eyes off Ben. "They were so relieved when the news got around that you were coming home."

"I will have to do something to thank everyone. There is no way I can ever repay their kindness for being worried about me." Tears pricked my eyes and I looked at the ceiling and blinked faster.

Chapter Thirty-One

ELLIE

August arrived faster than I could have imagined. Jessica had been over almost every day finalizing plans for our wedding, which would take place in five days. I had asked that nothing crazy be planned for the bachelorette party because I wasn't really a bachelorette, but Kate and Jessica both said it was a rite of passage.

Outwardly I groaned but inside my heart soared. Their small kindnesses made me feel accepted.

"Knock, knock." Sandra's voice rang out as she popped her head in the door. "Can I come in?"

"Absolutely. I'm in the living room," I called out from where I was nursing Ben on the couch.

"Oh, there's my perfect little man." Sandra took Ben when I held him out to her. "I think you're ready for a burp. Grandma has perfect timing." She sat down in the chair across from me and rocked him as she patted his back.

"Now, what do I need to know?" she asked quietly.

"I left you a list in the diaper bag. You have more than enough milk for the time we're gone." I trailed off, nervous about being away from him.

"Ellie, it's only overnight. You're just going to San Antonio and can be back here in no time. Between Kate's mom and Brian and me, everything will be in order." Sandra rested her cheek on the top of Ben's head.

Kate's mom, Julie, lived so close that she was a bonus grandma to all the Morton kids. She loved each of them like they were her own, and we were lucky to be able to call on her when we needed an extra set of hands.

Sandra and I were lost in conversation when Kate, Jessica, and Delaney waltzed through the door. "Are you ready to kiss your married days goodbye?" Kate asked. "That sounded so much better in my head. We will go out and come back in so I can try again."

Laughing, I shook my head. "It was cute." Even I couldn't make that sound convincing, and the other women laughed.

"All right, girls, get going. This little man and I are going home. Have a fun time." Sandra stood, buckled Ben in the stroller, and headed for the main house.

The day flew by. We shopped, we ate, and we laughed until our stomachs hurt. Then we Ubered back to the hotel to get ready for our night on the town.

We ended up at a bar where the music was loud and the room hazy from the smoke machine. Finding a table was difficult, but Kate's eagle eyes spotted one. Drinks in hand, we made our way to it.

"Care to dance, little lady?" A voice came from over my shoulder. The girls' eyes were as big as dinner plates, and they looked like they were about to burst with laughter. Turning, I stared into the face of a cowboy I knew.

"Yes, I'll dance with you," I said as I set down my drink.

The man helped me off the chair and guided me to the middle of the crowded dance floor.

"What are you doing here?" I asked.

Leaning down, he kissed me as we whirled around the floor. "Have you heard from Mom? Is Ben doing all right?"

Of course he would be more worried about Ben than he was about answering my questions.

"He's perfect. I called her just before we got here. She says it's like he has no idea we're even gone." Smiling, I moved closer to him when I slow song started. "Do you think they all planned this? Making sure we ended up here tonight?"

Gavin turned to look at the table. "Judging from the looks on their faces, absolutely. Are you okay with your party ending this way?"

"I wouldn't want it any other way," I said as he held me tighter.

When we were tired of dancing, we went to the table. We talked and laughed with our family, and I couldn't help but send up a little thank-you to the man upstairs.

After a little while, Gavin leaned down and whispered in my ear. "I have my own room at the hotel. Let's leave."

Downing the last of my drink, I looked at the group. "Thanks for the party, ladies, but I just got a better offer." I grabbed my purse and stood.

The girls hooted and hollered as we turned to go.

Gavin flopped down on the bed, arms outstretched, and sighed. "I don't think I've ever been happier to be somewhere this quiet."

I knelt and straddled the man splayed out before me. "It's nice but I wouldn't mind filling this room with a little noise," I murmured, leaning in, and kissing him passionately

Gavin moved his arms and let his hands rest on my ass. Kissing me until we both needed to stop for air, he rolled over and pinned me under him. "My wife isn't going to be happy I picked a woman up at the bar," he teased as he undid the top button of my blouse.

"For your sake, I hope she doesn't find out." My voice was husky as I played along.

Once my shirt was open, Gavin traced the hem of the bra with his finger, ever so lightly touching my skin. "This is new."

"I got it today. Do you like it?" Arching my brow, I pushed out my chest for him to have a better view.

"I'd like it better if it was on the floor." He pulled the sheer fabric down and put his mouth over my nipple.

Sighing with pleasure, I reached behind me and popped open the clasp. The bra came away from my breasts, and Gavin pulled it off.

He slid his hand from my breast down my stomach to the hem of the skirt I wore. Lifting my skirt to my hips, he finally found his target. The heat from his hand radiated through my thin panties.

"You need to wear short skirts more often," he mumbled into my ear.

Laughter erupted from me. "Gavin, we live on a cattle ranch, and we have a four-month-old. Short skirts aren't exactly practical."

"I'm not worried about practical. It's the ease of access I'm enjoying." Scooting down, he took my painfully hard nipple between his teeth and bit down gently.

Something wet fell on my arm, and I looked down to see a steady drip from the breast not being taken care of by Gavin. "Oh no. I should have pumped. Stop, and I'll do it now."

He looked up and grinned. "No, I'm not stopping. Tonight's the only night I don't have to share you. I love Ben, but this," he ran his hand over my breasts dragging the wetness across them and down my stomach to between my thighs, "is all mine tonight. Dripping tits and all." Moving my panties to the side, he slipped his fingers inside me and attacked my chest again.

Moaning, I ran my hands through his hair and arched my back. I needed more. Now.

"How do I get this skirt off?" Gavin said, tugging at my waistband.

I grabbed the zipper on the front of the skirt and dragged it down ever so slowly. "You wanted ease of access? Well, here it is."

Gavin watched me shimmy out of it with the biggest smile on his face. "This is now in the clothing rotation. Could you imagine the fun we could have at any moment?" His eyes glimmered.

I was still always amazed at his excitement for my body. I was taught to cover up and not tempt men. But Gavin worshipped every part of me, and it didn't matter what I was wearing or that I'd so recently given birth.

I was completely loved and in love with him. Nothing could have prepared me for the absolute joy that becoming his wife and a mother had given me. At one point in my life, I thought the only way I could be happy was to have a man in my life. It didn't matter what man. Now I realize the only reason I was happy was because Gavin made me feel like an equal. He believed in me and made sure I knew he was completely in love with me. Working together, trusting each other, and being partners in every sense of the word.

Chapter Thirty-Two

GAVIN

We were up with the sun yet again. Ben was the alarm clock that had the power to get everyone out of bed.

I went to the kitchen while Ellie went to get the baby. Opening the can of coffee and taking a deep breath always energized me, but this morning I would have liked to crawl back into bed.

Yesterday was the most perfect day. It was something I never thought would happen, but meeting this woman ten months ago changed everything. I had been happy being alone. Nobody needed me and required me to be better than I was. But now the beautiful woman upstairs and our son relied on me and I relied on them.

The coffee was done, so I poured two cups and climbed the stairs to Ben's room. Ellie was sitting in the rocking chair feeding our growing boy.

Ellie was stunning all the time, but when she was tenderly humming to Ben while he was eating, my heart filled with pride and love.

"Are you going to stand at the door all morning, or do I get that cup of coffee?" She never took her eyes off Ben but smiled softly as I approached.

Leaning down as she raised her head, I brushed my lips against hers. "Good morning," I whispered when we pulled away from each other.

She reached for the coffee and took a sip. Closing her eyes and savoring the first sip, she smiled. "Good morning. How did you sleep?"

"Like a rock, you?" I sat in the chair next to her and sighed. Spending time with my family was my number one priority, so we'd put two rocking chairs in the nursery so Ellie and I could talk while she was feeding Ben.

"Good, but I could have used a couple more hours of sleep." She arched her brow and smiled slyly.

"It was short, that's true but oh what a night." Lifting my mug, I took a sip of my coffee, never breaking eye contact with my wife.

Her sly smile turned shy as she looked back down to Ben. She shifted in the chair, stood, and walked to me. "He's done. You're on burping duty." Ellie shifted Ben in her arms, and I reached out to take him.

While Ellie bonded with the baby while feeding him, this was my time, and I treasured every moment of it.

Ellie backed up and looked at the two of us, her robe open so I got an eyeful of her gorgeous tits.

When she caught me staring at her chest, she reached for her robe, but I stopped her before she could cover herself up.

"Leave it. I like the view." Wiggling my eyebrows, I reached for the coffee I had set down before Ellie handed Ben over.

She had grown more comfortable with me and her body over the last few months. After Ben was born, she covered herself with a blanket while she nursed him, even at home. But lately, she had forgone the blanket.

"I think you saw them enough last night," she quipped, but she stepped closer.

"Baby, if you wandered around topless every day, and I spent all my time with my eyes glued to you, it still wouldn't be enough." I brushed my thumb over her nipple. The quick, breathy moan would have been easy to miss if she hadn't been so close to me.

She blushed and took a step back. "I'm going to get ready. What time do we leave?" she asked as she walked out of the room.

"You know naked would be preferred, because this view is another one of my favorites," I called after her.

She peeked back into the room. "Nice try. Focus, Gavin. Leaving. What time?"

"An hour and a half." Ben burped, and my job was done. He had fallen back to sleep, so I laid him back down in his crib, then met my wife at the nursery door. "Plenty of time to have a little fun of our own."

"Down, big fella. I have to shower and pack. Alone." She walked to the bathroom and closed the door, but she didn't flip the lock. I put my hand on the knob, but thought maybe she really did want privacy, so I turned to head back to our room to pack my bag.

"You coming or not?" My wife leaned against the doorframe, naked and with the biggest grin on her face.

She didn't have to ask me twice; I spun around and followed her back to the shower.

An hour and a half later, after frantically packing, we made it out the door on time.

"This is your fault," I said as we sat in our seats and waited for takeoff.

"Right. I had a plan, and you ruined it with all your dirty talk." Her voice dropped to a whisper.

"I didn't hear you complaining." I slid my hand up her leg and rested it on her inner thigh. "You know we could still join the mile high club."

"Gavin." She whispered and shook her head. "Don't you not think of anything else?"

"Well, when you're not around I can, but damn baby, you're hot and you're mine."

Just as I was about to attack her mouth, the flight attendant announced that we were ready for takeoff. "I will finish that thought later."

"I'm sure you will." She rolled her eyes and changed the subject. "I should nurse Ben so the takeoff doesn't bother him." Ellie unbuckled him and settled him on her lap.

I had managed to keep our location a secret. Not because she would be mad, but because I didn't want her to worry about it. "Want me to tell you where we're going?"

"Yes. You know I hate surprises." Ellie never took her eyes off Ben.

"Montana."

Her head shot up, and her mouth hung open. "Why?" She asked.

"Because I want to make new memories there. Good memories Only a handful of people know we are coming, and we will hide at the cabin, go hiking, enjoy our time with Ben." This might not have been the best idea I had ever had, but the plan had already been set in motion. "It's our place, Ellie. It's where we met. I want it to be our escape from Texas when we need a break from the chaos of life."

She nodded and smiled. "Okay. I trust you. I really am the luckiest woman alive."

I leaned in and took the kiss that I had put off moments ago. Kissing this woman for the rest of my life was the only thing I ever needed.

Epilogue

ELLIE

Gavin and I had lived on the ranch for five years. It was wonderful being so close to our loving family, but it was also overwhelming at times. I had moments of feeling like I was back on the compound, where everyone knew everyone else's business. There were many days I had to remind myself that this was different.

Ben was Gavin's shadow. He couldn't go anywhere without his son following. Cattle were Ben's passion, and the men of the Morton ranch were more than happy to teach him everything they knew.

New Dream Homes was busier than ever. We had gotten exposure from some news articles and television segments, so I was getting calls from all over the country to book builds and give walkthroughs of our model homes.

I stood at the fence, watching Kate work with one of the young barrel riders. She was so patient and focused on making sure the girls were learning proper techniques, not just speed.

A warm arm wrapped around my waist and rubbed my very pregnant belly. Leaning back into my husband was something I never got tired of.

"How are my girls doing?" He asked as he nibbled at my neck.

"Tired. Ready to meet each other." I sighed as he wrapped both arms under my baby bump and gently lifted to take the pressure off my back.

"Well, her daddy is getting anxious to meet her too," he whispered. "I hope it's not much longer."

"Me too, baby." We watched the horse run, his muscles powerful and beautiful.

"Happy anniversary."

"Gavin, it's not our anniversary until tomorrow," I said, shaking my head.

"Oh, how quickly you forget, my love. Today is the day I set this entire thing in motion. Forced you to fall in love with me." He let out a little chuckle.

Turning in his arms wasn't easy anymore, and I longed to not have this barrier between us.

"You did more than force me to fall in love with you. Gavin, you saved me from things I have tried not to think about over the years." Closing my eyes, I leaned my head on his shoulder. "Until the day I stumbled into your cabin, I was sure the only thing for me in life was death. I will be forever in your debt for that night."

Standing on my tiptoes, I kissed him. Just as our lips met, my stomach cramped like someone had punched me, and I let out a groan.

"Well, that wasn't quite the reaction I was expecting." Gavin frowned.

"Your daughter will be making her appearance today, I think." Squeezing my eyes shut, I breathed through another contraction.

"Are you serious?" Gavin's eyes were wild. He scanned the yard.

"Yes. It's time." Nodding, I walked around him and headed to the house.

"Kate, we have to go. Ben is with Tyler," Gavin yelled over to his sister-in-law.

"I'll get him. Good luck," Kate called.

I turned and waved, wishing she could come with me, but she and Tyler would keep Ben occupied.

Gavin drove to the hospital like he was in a high-speed chase. Laser focused and on a mission. The doctor had warned us that this delivery may be difficult given the trauma I endured after the accident, so we needed to get to the hospital as soon as possible.

At the hospital, the nurses had me registered and in my birthing room in less than fifteen minutes. Now we just had to wait for the doctor.

"Hi, Elyse. Looks like it's time for you to have this baby." Dr. Caver walked in, looking at a chart.

"I think so." I grinned. I felt good. The epidural was doing its job, and I hadn't felt a contraction for half an hour.

"I'll just do a quick check, and if all is good, you'll have this baby soon." She rolled a stool to the foot of my bed and folded the blanket up over my knees. Her mood went from friendly to all business instantly. "This little girl is impatient and has quite the head of hair," she said. "You're ready to push."

The nurse helped her prep the bed for delivery, and then Dr. Caver was giving out instructions.

"Okay. The nurse is going to hold one of your legs so you don't have to do all the work yourself. And Gavin, you'll hold the other." She gestured to him, and he mimicked the way the nurse looped an arm under my knee. "I'll tell you when to push."

I had completely missed Ben's delivery. When I arrived at the hospital, I was taken to the operating room and put under anesthesia so they could take Ben and fix the internal bleeding the accident had caused.

When the doctor signaled, I grabbed Gavin's hand and pushed with all my might.

"That's good. Stop for a minute."

My heart rate raced while I waited for further instruction. I wanted to know what was happening, and I felt like I was off in Lala land.

"One last big push."

I bared down with all my might, and what felt like seconds later, the cry of our daughter reverberated through the room.

"She's perfect." The doctor beamed as she placed the baby on my chest.

I couldn't help my tears. Everything around bringing Ben into the world had been traumatic. The joy I should have experienced had been taken from me. But this was perfect.

Gavin squeezed my hand and stroked our daughter's cheek with the back of one finger while tears flowing down his cheeks.

"Do you have a name picked out?" The nurse asked quietly.

"Hallie Sandra." Gavin and I said in unison.

"That's beautiful." The nurse replied as she reached to take my daughter off my chest. "We have a few things to do, but I promise I'll return little Hallie in a few minutes."

With Hallie in the nurse's hands, Gavin leaned downed kissed me. "Good job, Momma."

My heart was about ready to burst. Five years ago, I'd run from people who were supposed to care for me and love me. But I had run to a man who actually did.

My family hadn't tried to contact me in all these years. But I had sent the baby announcement to them when Ben was born anyway. And I would do the same with Hallie. They might not care that they were missing out on their grandchildren's lives, but I wasn't going to be the one that made it okay. So, every chance I got, I would let them know.

Life wasn't always easy, but it was far better than where I'd come from.

Gavin broke our kiss and smiled at me. "How many times are we doing this?"

"Kissing or the babies? Because I will happily kiss you for the rest of my life. But I think we're at our limit for babies. They won't outnumber us if we stick to two." I yawned.

Gavin kissed my forehead. "Rest, my love, I will check on Hallie."

I nodded and closed my eyes, quickly succumbing to sleep.

Out of despair, I ended up with the most beautiful life. I felt like a butterfly who had just emerged from its chrysalis. Unfolding its wings and taking flight for the first time.

Excerpt from The Arrangement

Chapter One

"You have got to be kidding! Why on earth would you think I would agree to something this insane?"

"I have no choice. I've got too much debt and borrowed from the wrong person. He's demanding payment." My father stood before me with hunched shoulders. His usual commanding voice was shaky, hesitant, and quiet.

"And the only decision you could think of was for me to marry one of his sons?" I shouted. Tears threatened to fall, but I willed them not to. I looked toward my mother, who hid behind my father; she sighed quietly and flitted her gaze to the ground whenever I looked at her. I had expected her to be arguing with me, or at least to appear angry, but she just stood there, holding on to my father's arm, patting it when he needed moral support.

The sun beat down on the parched earth stretching between us. I have welcomed shade, except there was not a cloud in the Texas sky. This conversation was only making me hotter; my temperature had risen at least five degrees since my dad opened his traitorous mouth. They'd both lost their damn minds. This couldn't be happening. My head was pounding and my brain felt like it was going to explode. There was no way I was going to agree to do something like this. Debt or no debt, I wasn't doing it.

"Brian Morton extended the option as a way out of my situation and to save our ranch. I don't have the money to pay him back."

"So you're going to sacrifice me? Use me as a pawn in your little game just so you can save this place? When did this ranch become more important than your daughter?" My voice was just above a whisper as I narrowed my eyes, staring a hole through my father.

He looked toward the ground and scuffed his boot along the gravel. "It's not more important," he disagrees, shaking his head, "but it's our family legacy. It's all I have to leave you one day." Tears filled his eyes, and he turned away from me so I wouldn't see. I could count on one hand how many times I'd seen my father cry. He was the picture of a rancher: tan, weathered face from years of being out in the elements, bowed legs from living on the back of a horse, and his black Stetson only came off for a meal, church service, or bed. Dad was always the level-headed one, the only man in a house full of women, so he learned early on how to solve arguments, heartache, and dodge hormones. He kept his feelings close to his vest. More often than not, you would have thought he didn't care, but that was just his way.

While I'd like to dismiss this crazy idea, I knew how much the ranch meant to him. He was a cowboy through and through. He even wrestled steers in his youth, which is how he met my mom, a rodeo queen in her own right. I worried that if he didn't have the ranch, he would lose part of himself. It was all he knew. Come to think of it, this was all I knew, and the thought of it not being here scared me. I turned away from my parents and wrapped my arms around my waist, closed my eyes, and allowed a few tears to fall. It hurt seeing him like this. It perplexed me how things had gotten this bad. When I came home to help, I thought things had turned around. Wiping my nose on my sleeve, I turned back around to face them.

"So if I do this, it takes care of all your debt?" The words came out far more confident than I felt. I knew if I agreed to this, I would be saving my father and losing myself.

My father nodded, closing his eyes in what I hoped was a silent prayer for my future.

My heart raced, and I began to pace in front of my parents. I fidgeted with my untucked shirt. I felt a wave of nausea hit me. Closing my eyes, I took a deep breath and waited for it to pass. I heard myself say, "Fine." I let out a loud sigh.

"So when am I supposed to get married?"

"A week and a half," Mom whispered as she stepped out from behind my father and took a few steps towards me. She tucked her blond hair behind her ear and clasped her hands in front of her, clearly bracing for my outburst like she had for years.

My mouth fell open, and it felt like my eyes would pop right out of my head. I stared at my mother and furrowed my brow, "Wow, you're sure not wasting any time getting rid of me."

A week and a half? They were as nuts as I thought. I looked at them both, waiting for something. Anything. Gratefulness? Praise, thanks or elation - but saw nothing. I turned on my heel and stomped away from them.

"Katherine Jean," my mom called after me, but I didn't stop. I didn't need to hear any more of this twisted bargain. There was nothing they could say that would make me feel better.

Chapter Two

I stomped off to the bunkhouse which was across the yard from my parents' house. Years ago I'd converted it to a little apartment, because I was the one who stayed. A whole lotta good that did me.

I paced around my kitchen. It wasn't very big, and the island took up the majority of the floor space. I got dizzy making laps around it. Slamming my hands down on the counter, I let the bottled up tears fall. I wanted to yell. I needed to hit something, or better yet, some*one*, but there was nobody. No one followed me, and that hurt almost as much as this convoluted arrangement. I snatched up a coffee mug that was beside the sink and threw it across the kitchen. It hit the doorjamb, shattered, and fell to the floor. Grumbling to myself, I grabbed the broom and bent down to sweep the china into the dustpan.

"Hey, Kate, it's nice to see you again." My eyes followed his legs up to his head and I saw Tyler Morton standing at the threshold of my home, too good to knock. Or maybe he thought that because we were an unofficial family, what was mine was his. Or I hadn't closed the door when I came home and it was an open invitation for him to come in. With him, who knew?

I had to admit; he was handsome. He was muscular; his eyes rivaled the clearest blue water, brown hair with highlights of gold from being in the sun, and the perfect amount of scruff on his unshaven face. It was just enough without encroaching on beard territory. And most importantly, he had the best Wrangler butt I'd ever seen.

"Hey, Tyler, come on in." I stepped out of the way and most definitely did not look at his butt as he walked by. Removing his ball cap, he sat down at the table. "Would you like a cup of coffee?"

"Sure, as long as the delivery is a little softer than what you used on that last cup." He smiled, and his eyes danced with laughter that he was smart enough to know not to let out.

"You saw that?" I cringed as I walked to the garbage can and dumped the broken cup. It clattered loudly as it hit the bottom of the can. The sound reverberated through my tiny house.

Tyler nodded. "Good throw."

"Do you know what's going on?" he asked, a little apprehensive.

"Kinda... wait. It's you?" I turned away from the counter, full pot of coffee in hand, barely avoiding splashing it, and looked at him. "You're the Morton brother I'm supposed to marry?"

He nodded his head, took a deep breath, and let it out slowly. What? Seriously? I'd had a secret crush on Tyler Morton since they moved here from Montana.

Carefully, I turned back to the counter to fill both cups. I looked out the window and fidgeted with the coffee pot, avoiding eye contact. My heart raced and palms suddenly sweaty. I thought back to the times I had seen him around. I had been too afraid to talk to him, and now here he was, in my kitchen, telling me we're going to be married. How was I supposed to pull myself back together to form sentences? I turned to face him again, took the cups back to the table, and went back for the milk and sugar.

"None for me, thanks. Black is good." Tyler shifted in the chair.

I smiled and walked back over to the table and took a seat across from him. "Did you just find out about this, too? It's a bit of a shock."

"No, our fathers wanted to keep this quiet. I told them there'd be no more hiding this from you and I was coming to see you today." Tyler took a sip of his coffee and waited for my response. "What's wrong?" The confused look on my face must have been more prominent than I thought.

"How long have you known about this?" I looked into my cup of coffee, refusing to meet his gaze.

"A week and a half."

My head shot up and my mouth fell open. I had so many words and questions, but not a sound came out. My eyes darted from my cup to Tyler as I searched my brain for the words. I felt like someone had slapped me across the face. This wasn't something that had just happened. Everyone around me knew the plan for weeks, and apparently, I wasn't good enough to be included. They had decided my life for me, and here I'd been wandering around, living what I thought was my best life, only to find out I'd been fooled. The world around me was out of control.

"Look, we've known each other for ten years now, it's not like we're complete strangers. It's not like we're going in blind."

"Tyler, you know who I am, but you don't know me." I pointed to myself.

He nodded his head and took another sip of his coffee.

"May I ask your expectations for this marriage?" All of the sudden, I wasn't sure I wanted to hear his answer. It frankly terrified me to actually know what he was going to say. My hands were folded in my lap. I needed to start thinking of this as what it was - a business deal. I straightened in my chair and took a deep breath, locking my stare on Tyler. I was ready to argue with anything he had to say.

Tyler peered over his mug and smiled. "I want to get to know you. Learn who you are, but ultimately, I want us to have a real marriage. You know, a true husband and wife."

"Well, I'll tell you that's not going to happen for a very long time. And I'm not hopping into bed with someone I've only really known for a week and a half. I'm not that kind of girl." My brow arched, waiting for his response.

"And for some reason, you think I'm that kind of guy?"

The town playboy, the eternal bachelor. He preferred busty blondes who wouldn't last on a working ranch. Yet he sat here, trying to convince me he was an angel.

I rolled my eyes before I glanced back over at him. "You kinda have a reputation. I may not know you all that well, but I've heard stories. Girl's talk."

"My reputation isn't something I can deny. There was a time in my life when I didn't give much thought as to who I was seeing, or how long we were together."

"Days, Tyler. Most of them were days."

"You seem to have kept tabs on me, Kate." A sly grin stretched across his face. He made my blood boil. He had the nerve to think that I had followed his every move? "That, I assure you, is not the case. It's a small town, Tyler, and gossip spreads faster than flies on a horse's ass."

"Well, I'm happy to be an open book; what would you like to know?"

I stared at him blankly, then shook my head. I dropped my face into my hands. This was not how I imagined my life would end up.

"This is too much, Tyler. I don't know if I can do this."

"You don't have to, but my father will not back down. I'm willing to marry you if you want to save your ranch, but ultimately it's your choice. Saying I'm totally thrilled about this would be a lie. I don't enjoy having choices made for me."

Really, I shouldn't have been surprised by his answer. That was the story of my life. I can't deny that it stung a little to know I wasn't who he wanted to be stuck with. "Well, I'm glad we both can agree this isn't the choice we would've made. I'm not sure I'll ever like it, Tyler. I've had about all I can take today. Thanks for coming over; I'll see you at the wedding."

He stood, walked to the door, and quietly left.

Acknowledgments

With the publishing of this book the Morton Family draws to a close.

Almost a year ago I hit publish on book one, The Arrangement and it was a dream come true.

Along the way people have come and gone that have helped me on this journey but one constant remains, Ashley.

You have become more than just a writing partner. You're a friend, encourager and a wonderful writer. Thank you for all the massive amounts of help on this book, you said from book one Gavin was your favourite brother and I hope I wrote him to your vision!

Beth, you have edited three of the four Morton books and your knowledge, and tough editing has made these stories better than I could think of. Thank you for your hard work.

JS Designs Covers, What can I say about the covers you have done for this series? You got my vision with The Arrangement right through to the cover for this book. You have been a joy to work with and I look forward to more of your covers on my books.

Readers, I hope you have enjoyed looking into this fictional family. I hope you have laughed, smiled or maybe even cried along the way. This might be the end for this series but it isn't the end of my writing. Keep an eye out for the Mountain Man books I am going to be publishing very soon.

About Author

Bonnie lives in South Central Saskatchewan in the heart of the Canadian prairies. She's married to Terence, who farms, ranches and is a hunting outfitter and guide in the northern part of the province. Terence and Bonnie have two children. Emerson is six and loves helping with the farm and cattle. Cassidy, who is three, is mom's shadow, talking a mile a minute and loves helping in the garden.

Bonnie has been a Licensed Practical Nurse for the last twenty years. She's worked in a busy city hospital, managed a long term care facility and is now working casually as a floor nurse to spend time at home raising the kids and helping on the farm.

When she's not writing, helping Terence and keeping the kids busy she enjoys vegetable gardening, tending to her flowers, reading and photography.

Stay up to date with what's happening in my world, and I will be releasing bonus content for some of my published works in the near future!

https://sendfox.com/bonniepoirier.author
Stay in touch with my author page on Facebook

https://www.facebook.com/bonniepoirierauthor

The Arrangement: The Morton Family Saga Book One
https://books2read.com/u/ba6xxa
The Atonement: The Morton Family Saga Book Two
https://books2read.com/u/31eool
The Assignment: The Morton Family Saga Novella
https://books2read.com/u/medxx9
A Time to Heal https://books2read.com/u/47Y61q